MAINSTRIP PUBLISHING PRESENTS........

Worth It

Written By:

Jay Mainstrip

MAINSTRIP PUBLISHING PRESENTS

Worth It

Chapter

1

Another hot ass morning is what woke me up. Even just stepping out of the shower, I still wasn't cool enough. The news predicted the weather to be ninety-six degrees and one of the hottest days of the summer. I swore that it had to be at least one hundred and fifty degrees inside our house. If I wanted to stay cool, I had to sit up under the fans without moving. Air Conditioning was not an option for my mother and I; If we wanted to stay cool, we had to do as the other families did. Close all of the blinds or shades, drink a lot of water, and move as little as possible.

I, on the other hand, could not stay still for long. I had to go to work a little later, so I needed to prepare. I was only fourteen years old and worked the late shift to make some money.

I stepped out of my bedroom summer dressed fresh wearing a crispy white t-shirt, basketball shorts, and some clean air Jordan that was only a couple months old. Tucked underneath the white t-shirt was my .40 caliber pistol that sat in its holster on my waistband. It was the only thing that my father had left me before being arrested and sentenced to life in prison. Most kids was in love with sports, video games, and girls, but I was different. I was in love with guns, bullets, and money; that's why I dropped out of school. Books did not feed my stomach; I had to get out and get it myself.

I opened up the refrigerator, hoping that some food was inside but was quickly disappointed as always. I headed out the door when my mother called my name from her bedroom, "Romello? Hey Romello?! You got some money?" She asked. I went back to her bedroom where she was barely able to sit herself up. She still had the clothes on from the night before. One high heel hung loosely on her foot, while clothes hung off her body. Even her hair was all over the place. I walked over sitting beside the mother that I loved so dearly but was totally disappointed with her, "Hey Ma, what time did you get in? Have you eaten?" I asked her while brushing the hair out of her face. Her lips were completely dry as she began to speak, "Huh? Yes, Baby, I ate, but I need some money so I could eat later on. You got some money?" She asked again. I exhaled, knowing that the money I was pulling out of my pocket would not go toward any food, no matter how much she was hungry.

The Cocaine and Heroin had taken a toll on my mother, and I hated it. My mother was a beautiful woman once upon a time and even used to be an R/N at the hospital, making close to a hundred thousand dollars a year. That was up until my father, who was a straight hood nigga from the Eastside of Detroit, exposed her to the real street life for real. My father was a *Certified Hitman*, in our neighborhood, they called him the *Boogie Man* from how he striked fear in people's hearts. When he took a big order on the city prosecutor, who was facing life for something totally different, he was given up by that same motherfucker in exchange for his own life. When my father was sentenced to life without the possibility of parole, it crushed my mother. She threw a *"Free Romello"* party were one of my father's fake friends got her by herself, laced her weed, and took her back to his house for days where he raped and drugged her until she fiend for more. By the time my mother showed back up, she had

?

been injected with so much heroin that she would never be the same. She lost her job, and ever since then, things have never been the same, she never told me who it was that drugged her either. That happened when I was eleven years old, and ever since then, I been living as an adult.

I handed my mother ten dollars, "Make sho' you eat Ma, do you hear me?" I asked her like she was my child instead of the other way around. She nodded her head with a smile.

"And I want you to go and get in the shower to get yourself together. Your pretty, and you should look like it." I told her as I headed out of her bedroom. She smiled, "Thank you, son, you take care of me just like your Daddy use too. I love you." She told me.

Hearing that I was doing something that reminded her of my Father also made me smile. "You have your gun on you right?" She asked me. I nodded my head answering yes and that I would see her later. "Hey Ma, I love you too,"

When I left out the house I pulled my bike from off the side of the house and hopped right on it hitting the streets. As I rode passed all of my neighbors, they all waved and spoke to me, they knew me since I was younger. The cars were riding down the block, blasting their music. Throwing up the deuces, some yelled my name as I rode past a couple of Trap Houses that had a porch full of niggas. They would always ask me if I was straight or needed something. The whole neighborhood loved me mainly because of the respect they had for my father, they knew he was never coming home but never wanted to get on his bad side under any circumstances because they know that he could still have people touched even from where he was. The other half of the neighborhood did not like me, and that probably meant that my father must have killed somebody in their family. Either way it went, they all still respected me but deep down inside, they hated the blood that flowed through my veins...

I rolled up to Dime's Chop Shop, where I would bring all of my stolen goods to sell when his Workers told me that he was not there. They paid me one hundred and fifty dollars a week. One hundred and fifty weekly was a lot to a fourteen-year-old boy, but it wasn't necessarily for me to splurge. I had to buy my own necessities like boxers, socks, and deodorant. I use to make a bit more than just the one hundred and fifty that I was paid by Dime. Whenever I would break into a car or a house, I always found more than I would report to him. I always found valuable things that I knew that I would get a lot of money for. The neighborhood Dope Boys were my main customers because they would buy almost anything from me, they even began requesting orders for things they wanted me to get.

"Man..these Niggas...Hey, walk wit' me for a second." Tiger told me as we walked away from his crew that was sitting on the porch. I looked back at Tiger, his brothers, and crew, and they all had a dumb look on their faces. Anytime they would try and clown me Tiger always took up for me. We walked up the block, walking with Tiger made me feel like I was walking with a celebrity. All the neighborhood hood-rats would wave and smile at him, and all of the niggas gave him respect like he was a type of mob boss. I liked walking with him because he would tell everybody that I was his little brother, so I was respected as well. "So, you think about what we talked about?" Tiger asked me. I nodded my head, "Yes, I thought about it, and I don't really know yet. I'm not a Killer like my old man was. That's what he did and how he made his name. I'm trying to make my own name out here, feel me? I answered him. Tiger had been trying to convince me to start taking hits like my father use to, but I wasn't really feeling it. He chuckled. "You trynna make a name doing what? Breaking in shit? Look, you can't keep breaking in people shit cause eventually a Motha'fucka is gon' catch you and try to kill yo' lil ass. I'm telling you, at least with me, you could make five thousand dollars a body versus making yo lil hundred and fifty dollars. Come and work for me, and I would get you paid. "Tiger told me.

Hearing that he would pay me five thousand dollars a body would be light way life-changing for me. I would be able to really take care of my Mother and try to get her out the streets. I would be able to buy us groceries and be able to actually fix us homemade meals like we were a real family. Standing there, thinking about how five thousand dollars would change my life, I quickly got side-tracked when I saw one of the prettiest girls I ever seen across the street. It was Madison who I use to go to school with before I dropped out, I had the biggest crush on her still to this day. As bad as I wanted her to be mine, it was damn near close to being impossible. To try and holler at her with the over-protective Brothers she had was slim to none. I hated all three of her Brothers, and they hated me.

Our families had generations worth of beef and animosity toward each other, and still to this day, no generation had put an end to it. The reason this generation hated me the most was because my father allegedly set their uncle up to be killed. Knowing who my father was, I knew that it was very possible. "Lil' Mello?! Hey, do you hear me?! Mello?!!" Tiger yelled at me, getting my attention. I snapped out of my daze. "What the hell you... Oh, I see.

you staring at lil' Madison over there and she got you gone. Uhhh, gon head lil bro. Go handle yo biz over there and Imma handle mines over here. I'll get wit' you, make sho you think about that five racks we talked about. It's in yo blood!!" Tiger told me as he gave me a play while running over to one of his customers. I told him I would think about it, and I rode my bike across the street where Madison was walking with her two friends. I pulled up behind Madison and her friends. "Whasup Madison?" I spoke with a smile on my face.

"Hey Romello, whasup' wit' You?" She asked with a smile on her face. "Oh, I ain't doing nothing. Just came from over here to holler at the big Bro Tiger then I saw you and had to come over and speak. "You looking good as usual." I complimented her using some of the young game I picked up on. "Thank you, you're not looking to bad yourself. I wish I could be like you and have the new Jordan's every week." She replied, checking me out. "Yo Romello, how you be having all this new stuff and you mama..." Candace, Madison's friend was asking until Madison nudged her hard enough to stop her from finishing her question.

It was no secret that my Mother was a Dope Fiend, but it has always been sensitive subject, and the one thing everybody in the neighborhood knew was that I would fight defending my family.

"Nawl, nawl, nawl Madison. Don't stop Candace from asking important questions, go ahead, ask him. I'll ask him then...How are you able to buy now Jordan's and stay clean as you do with a Father serving life in prison and a crackhead, mama? I'll tell yall how he do it... Its cuz all he do is break in people's houses and cars to get money, that's how!" Madison's older Brother Nate said, stepping off of the porch and into the circle mugging me. I stood there with my blood boiling as Nate, and I had a stare-off, "Madison, I'll see you later." I said, turning to walk away before I snapped. "No, you won't Nigga! Do I come and visit yo' Crackhead Ass Mama at the Crack House?! No, so don't come and visit my Sister!" Nate yelled.

While I walked away I stopped in my tracks, hearing enough insults from Nate. I turned around facing Nate when I noticed that the entire neighborhood was watching, including Tiger and his Brothers. Tiger gave me the head nod signaling me like I better had handled the situation, and indeed I was. At that moment, I went into a different zone, and Nate's Brothers and Father standing on the porch didn't faze me, Madison standing there with a worried look on her face didn't faze me either. I had tunnel vision with no background sound included, and the only thing that I was focused on was beating Nate's Ass

⍰

for his disrespectful comments. I ran up on Him without giving him a chance to prepare. I hit him with the quickest six-piece combo all to the face that instantly sent him falling to the grass in pain. I jumped on top of him, blessing him with the hard-hitting fist that God had blessed me with, and all he could do was accept the blessing.

Nate's Brothers jumped off of the porch, snatching me off their beat up Brother Nate and slinging Me to the ground beside him. They both began punching and stomping me while I was on the ground. They pulled me out of my tunnel vision, and all I could hear was the cheers from their friends, Madison screaming for them to stop and get off of Me and last but not least, I heard their Father cheering his boys on to beat Me up. Knowing that I was outnumbered, Tiger and his Brother began cheering for me to get up and to fight back. All the anger I had plus the cheers from both parties had encouraged me to fight back, and just like that, I had gained the strength to knock all of them off the top of Me. I slid back while still on the ground separating Myself from them when I pulled out my .40 caliber pistol aiming it at all of them demanding that they stayed back. All of them stayed still raising their hands to the sky. Madison helped her Brother Nate to his feet and the entire neighborhood was silent watching and waiting on my next move. I was pissed as I wiped the blood from my busted lip.

"C'mon boys, yall already whooped his ass, it's time to come inside and get cleaned up. Good job, I'm proud of yall." their Father told them. They all retreated back into the house, including Madison, "And you. You stay away from my Daughter, or I'll kill you Myself. Got me!?" The Father threatened me. I lowered my gun when I heard their Father tell them that's why my Mother was a Crackhead and Father serving a life bit. He said to them that I would be following in my parent's footsteps. Madison stood in the front door staring at me with a look that I been getting all of my life, the pity look. She then closed the door as I stood there, still fuming in anger.

I tucked my pistol back in my pants, hopped back on my bike, and rode off in the direction of Tiger's Trap House. He called my name and stopped me, "Yo', next time you pull yo' gun out, you betta' use it! You hear me?! You betta' use it! Hey... But you did good other than that. Keep yo' head up, Boy!" Tiger told me, giving me a play. I rode away feeling good that Tiger was proud of me, but I knew that Nate wouldn't let this situation go without a second round being that I whooped his ass. I'll be ready...

2

Get Back

ONE WEEK LATER

A week had passed since I whooped Madison's brother ass, and was jumped by her Brother's, yet I still was not even tripping. I was more focused on getting this money out in these streets, and the five thousand a body payment that Tiger was telling me about was seriously being considered. Between my mother needing to shake her drug habit and from our house falling apart. We both needed a change, and that five thousand would be a huge help. The little hundred and fifty dollars that I was making stealing shit for Dime was no longer helping, and I needed some serious cash. Something was going to have to shake, but for now, the hundred and fifty dollars that I had was going to have to buy my Mother and me some groceries so that we could eat tonight.

I walked inside the grocery store to buy a few items, and to my surprise, Madison was at the cash register paying for her things. Seeing Madison always bought butterflies to my stomach and sent my hormones into a frenzy. I saw a concerning look on Madison's face as she stood there, the cashier looked irritated at the fact she didn't have enough money. Three people stood behind Madison in line with the same annoyed face. I excused myself and walked passed all of them, "Madison, whasup? You aight?" I asked. When she saw me, she had a look of relief.

"Oh, hey, Romello? Ummm! I must've lost my money on the way here, or something my daddy is going to kill me! I don't.." She tried explaining when I stopped her and asked how much the difference was the cashier answered for her, "$46.32." Without hesitation, I reached in my pocket and paid her total. Knowing that I was helping feed her family most definitely was not on my to-do list, but I knew how Madison's father would beat her if he found out that she lost the grocery money, so I helped the

🔲

only way that I knew how. We walked down the street, both carrying our groceries when Madison thanked me for buying her family's groceries, "You know, I wanted to apologize for my stupid brother's jumping on you the other day. Their very over-protective and stupid at the same time, the things that they said about your family...She was saying until I cut her off. "You don't have to apologize for your brothers, it's true. My mother is a dope fiend, and my old man is serving life in the joint, that's just what it is. One thing about it is I guarantee that the I be great in the future." I replied. She smiled, impressed by my answer, "And what is your plan to be great? Madison asked me. I paused before answering, "You might think that it's funny, but I wanna' go to college, and if everything goes right, I want to become a writer. I know it's crazy, but I'm actually good and that has always been a goal of mine to do." I told her.

I looked over at Madison while we walked and she had a serious look on her face, "Romello, nothing is funny or crazy about your plans, I believe that you could do it and become a great writer someday. You just have to stay focused," Madison told me. I then asked her what she wanted to grow up and be. She answered a doctor. "Somebody has to be the doctor in the family to patch my brother's up when they get beat up." She said, bumping elbows with me and grinning.

"Where did you learn to fight like that, by the way? You got hands, Boy! If my Brother's seen Me walking with you you're going to need em again because Nate was pissed and still is." She told me.

"Awww, Nate would be aight. And my Father taught me how to fight the way I do, shoot guns, and just how to be a Survivor." I answered Her.

"Oh shit, damn! There are all three of my Brothers!! Tell me that you have your gun on you because at least that would scare them. "Madison asked with a worried look on her face. I patted my waistband where I always kept my pistol when I realized that I had left it at home, so it didn't fall down my shorts while I carried the groceries. I told Madison that I left it at home she shook her head, "Well, I think that you should go the other way because my Brother Nate wants revenge!" She told me. One of the things that my Father taught me was when things got thick that a real man never runs but faces like a real man would.

"Nawl I won't be doing that, but if this is what he's looking for, then this is what Imma' give him. I suggest you go and find some help because shit is about to get real for one of us. I told her never taking my eye off my Enemies that were approaching. Madison walked up to her brother Nate trying to talk him down from starting something, but he was not trying to hear it. He pushed her to his other brothers, "Didn't pops tell you to stay away from him?! Didn't we tell you to stay away from him too?! Go home, Madison! Go Home now!" Nate yelled at her.

Madison quickly ran home, knowing that things were going to get real serious. Nate and I both squared off, "You snuck me last time Mello, this time imma' beat the shit outta' you!" Nate said, getting himself ready with a fake ass mug on his face. I put down the groceries and exhaled, "Look, Nate, I ain't even trying to fight you," I told him in the humblest way possible, but soon as I finished my sentence, she rushed me swinging hard and missed. His brothers Man-Man and Stone surrounded us while cheering their brother on when I threw a quick jab to his nose. He swung again missing me, I hit him with another quick jab to the nose that made his head jerk back. Behind Nate and his Brothers, I saw Tiger's Box Chevy Caprice turn the corner and park a few feet away. Seeing Tiger was straight motivation for me to handle my business. With Nate's nose already bleeding, he charged at me, catching a quick four-piece combination that made his knees buckle and dropped him where he stood. Their Father and Madison had rushed around the corner, just witnessing the beating that I was putting on their own when the father yelled for his brothers to jump in and help, and they did.

For the first few minutes, I was putting up a good fight whooping on both of the brothers at the same time until Nate finally came to. He picked up a two by four log of wood that was in front of someone's yard and went across my back with it dropping me to the ground. All three of them began stomping me hard while was down on the ground. Again I was hearing their father cheer his boys on and for them to keep going, Madison was screaming for them to stop and the big difference between the last time and this time was that they were seriously causing some damage. I was in pain from the heavy kicks, and I remembered badly wanting them to stop. All of a sudden, a loud gunshot was fired making everybody jump from and had everybody looking around wondering who was shooting. When I looked up and seen Tiger walking toward me with his pistol in his hand, I damn near dropped a tear of joy to see him. He mugged Madison's family, telling them to go home, and without an argument or debate, they started walking away. "Yea Bitch, This shit is going to happen every time I see you!" Nate threatened as he limped away with a swollen face. Tiger stood over me, helping me to my feet, but I could barely stand.

?

"Damn Lil' Mello, I can't even lie. You got them Hands! You were fuckin' them up, a nice minute," Tiger said with an impressed smile on his face while he helped me over to his car, "Yea? I sho' could've used your help when you see that big ass two by four hit me!" I told him. He laughed, "Yo! Bro, my shoulder...My shoulder don't feel right, it feels like it's outta' place." I said as I leaned over. Tiger took a look at my shoulder and told me that it was dislocated. He told me to stay still while he put it back in its place, "Ahhh!!" I yelled from the pain. We hopped in the car and pulled off, "So whatchu' gon' do bout' them fuckin' you up? I know you're not gon' just let that shit keep riding. Tiger asked me.

Holding on to my injured shoulder, I could not help but to be mad at the situation. Did they think that they could jump me, and I wouldn't do anything? Them niggas were going to pay, and Nate would be the first one to get it the worst. "Hell Nawl I ain't letting that shit ride! I got something for them." I answered Tiger.....

3

THE PLOT

Five Days Later

After a couple of days of healing from the beating that I had taken, I was still furious as if it had just happened. My knee was swollen from the many stomps I took and with my shoulder being in as much pain as it was in, I couldn't even get out to make myself any money. Luckily my mother had not been home in days, so I only had to take care of myself, which was hard enough. I was still pissed that I had been jumped twice, but I was still also worried about my mother, who disappeared as she did often but not for five days straight. I was use to her frequent disappearing, so I tried not to worry as much but to concentrate on how I would handle Madison's Brothers.

In a couple of days that it took me to heal from the beating that I received, I took the time to think of the best plan on how I would get my revenge on her Brothers. For starters, I knew that my first step was taking Nate out of the picture. The anger I had toward Nate and his family made the thought of killing him very logical. If I killed Nate, then his brothers would be lost and running around like chicken with their heads chopped off. They would no longer have a leader, no longer be a threat toward me, and I would no longer have to kill them.

Yes, I would be the number one suspect, but the only brother that would ever confront me about it was Man-Man. He was the dumb Hothead Brother that would be Quick to act without a plan, which was one of the quickest ways to get himself killed. I began to plot on what I would do, and I figured out that the best time to execute my plan was to catch Nate when he walked up to the corner liquor store when his father would have him and pick up his daily store items he got at the same time every night. I was officially going to kill Nate for becoming a cancer in my life, and that badly needed to be removed. This would be my first time murdering someone, and even though I was serious. considering accepting Tiger's five thousand hit I refused to follow in my father's footsteps. I then vowed that Nate would be the first and only boy that I would place into a grave, now I just needed a plan....

✳ ✳ ✳

(10:15pm)

It was another hot and humid Saturday night as I laid in the bushes of an abandoned house. It sat two houses away from the corner liquor store and two blocks away from Nate and Madison's house where he would be coming from. Wearing my all-black attire with the *Scream* mask on my face and my .40 caliber pistol in my hand cocked and loaded, it was almost game time. The rats were scurrying pass me, the mosquitos were biting me, and that was not even the worst part. The worst part was noticing just how crowded the liquor store was tonight. It seemed like everybody from the neighborhood was hanging and posting in the parking lot. I even saw Tiger parked ducked off behind the liquor store in the alleyway. Clearly, the liquor store was where everybody was hanging, so I most definitely could not kill Nate there. The best place to do it would be between the liquor store and the corner house in the alleyway. I would have to move swiftly in and out so I wouldn't be detected by any witnesses or nosy ass neighbors.

I stared up the block waiting on Nate to head my way, and when I saw him coming he made my heart beat harder than it usually did. When I seen Madison catch up with him so she could join him, my heart damn near jumped out of my chest. I automatically began to panic and became confused as to how I would handle this now. I planned on killing Nate. I didn't plan on killing him with his Sister beside him. I couldn't do that to Madison, her brother being killed would already be a hard pill to swallow but witnessing it would be even harder. I crept out of the bushes ready to abort the mission and removing my mask when I heard a familiar voice call my name, I turned around, and it was Tiger standing beside his car, where I planned on catching Nate walking by. "A Dog, Lil' Mello. . What is you doing? you look like you're on some bullsh... "He was saying until he saw the pistol and mask in my hand. Tiger began looking around seeing what I was up to, and when he saw Nate and Madison heading our way, he just nodded his head with a grin on his face.

"Ohh okay. Do yo' thang Lil' Bro and make sho' your careful. Go do dat' shit! That nigga and his bros jumped you a couple of times, and you can't let that shit ride. He's gotta' pay! That killing shit is in your blood, make me proud! Imma' be right parked right over there just in case shit gets real and you need me. Handle that shit Lil' Bro!" Tiger said, motivating me. Tiger was far from stupid, when he seen me dressed in my all black with mask and gun in hand, he already knew that I was about to put a play down. After Tiger's motivating words, I jumped right back in the bushes and was ready to take care of the business that needed to be handled, and I disregarded Madison being by his side.

With Tiger getting in his position away from where I was hiding. Nate and Madison unknowingly walking passed where I was hiding, I couldn't wait until they came back out from the liquor store. I then snuck out of the bushes and over into the alleyway where I would hide behind the garbage cans. I kneeled down and was patiently waiting to hit Nate with the attack he has never seen in his life. It was a bit weird to me how I was so very comfortable, calm, and relaxed, being that I was about to kill somebody. I began to wonder if my father was ever this comfortable before he went on his killing Sprees.

From about a good fifteen feet away from where Nate and his sister would be bypassing, the loud and distinct voice of Nate irritated my skin when I heard him threatening his sister that if he caught her with me again that he would whoop her worse than what their father did to them. Hearing Nate threaten his sister and that their father punished her for being around me only added more fuel to the fire that I was directing toward Nate. I closed my eyes, exhaled, and counted to three. "Okay, let's do this!" I whispered to myself before running from behind the garbage can.

Both Madison and Nate walked passed the alleyway, where I was hiding when I quickly ran up on them from behind, "Hey!!" I yelled in a changed voice with pistol aimed at Nate's head. They both turned around, and when Madison seen the gun aimed at her brother her automatic reaction was to scream to the top of her lungs.

Nate was actually tougher than I expected him to be, "Oh yeah? You so much of a pussy you have to kill me with a mask on?!" Nate said to me. I stood there so badly wanting to take the mask off to show him who was ending his life, but I couldn't let him get under my skin. Remembering how him and his brothers jumped me, I pulled the trigger sending a bullet through his forehead and watched his body slowly fall to the ground. The streets were completely silent. Even I was in a different zone after what I had just done. When his body hit the ground, I added another three shots. Standing there watching Nate take his last breath, I then looked up at Madison who stared down at her brother's lifeless body she was speechless. She then looked up at me and instantly bouncing over toward me, screaming, yelling, and trying to remove my mask from my face.

Realizing what I had just done, It was time for me to get far away from here but Madison jumping on my back was slowing me down. All the neighbors began coming outside when they heard Madison's screams, and they cheered for her to hold on to me tight. While on my back Madison still attempting to take my mask off, it was time for me to shake her off and get out of there. I began throwing elbows to her ribs, and one of them hit her in the face sending her to the ground in pain. When I noticed how I had just dropped the girl I cared for my entire life, I kneeled down beside her.

"Madison?!" I said, worried if she was seriously hurt. Madison had been knocked dizzy and was totally confused as to what was going on. The police sirens began wailing and echoing throughout the neighborhood, reminding me just how serious things were at the time. I then took off down the block when I heard neighbors pointing me out to the police and to Nate's Brother's that had gotten a word in what had just happened. I wasn't only running from the police, but now I was dodging her brother's and the neighborhood good Samaritans. I was in a tight bind but being that I knew the neighborhood as well as I did, I was giving the police and her brother's a run for their money.

Running through a neighborhood with a mask on my face was not hard to miss, but it was a must that I kept it on to conceal my identity. Using all of my energy refusing to be caught, I ended back up toward the liquor store, where I remembered Tiger was. When I saw his car was still parked in the same spot, I quickly ran toward him, who was already standing by the trunk. "Let me guess, you trynna' get outta' here?.. I thought so, get in!"
He told me, lifting up his trunk for me to hop in. Confused and not knowing what was going on, Tiger looked at me like I was crazy. "Get in Nigga! I know you don't think you would ride in the front with me with as many police that's
in the hood cuz' of yo hot-ass! Hop in!" He yelled.

Hearing all of the police sirens through the neighborhood, being chased by the good Samaritans and Nate's brothers hot on my trail, I didn't have much of a choice but to get in or get caught. Since being caught was not an option I hopped in Tiger's trunk, he closed it behind me, and he pulled off. Tiger was the real O.G in my neighborhood and all, but I was still skeptical on fully trusting him. One of the rules that my father taught me was to trust no one, but I did the moment that I jumped in his trunk. If he wanted to, he could have turned me into the police or to

Nate's Brothers and Father. I hated how my future was in Tiger's hands, but I had to deal with it under the circumstances....

***

(TWENTY MINUTES LATER)

I felt Tiger's car come to a complete stop when I prepared for whatever and whoever to be waiting for me when the trunk opened. With my pistol in hand aimed forward, Tiger popped the trunk open and couldn't help but to chuckle after seeing how paranoid I was. He walked away and told me to follow him inside the house. I stepped out of the trunk unfamiliar with the neighborhood we were in. All I knew was that we were still in Detroit. Hoodrats walking up and down the streets. Old people sitting on their porches and cars were riding down the block with their sounds pounding was all that I was seeing.

When I stepped into the house, it was decked out with some of the best furniture and appliances. New flat-screen televisions, the fresh paint smell, and brand-new carpet had been laid down."Ummm, what sizes are you Lil'

?

Mello? Bout a thirty-eight in pants, two XL shirt?" Tiger asked. I nodded my head yes and asked why, which he then told me to go to the back bedroom, where there would be everything that I needed brand new. He told me to go and hop in the shower and when I was finished that he would be chilling out on the couch so we could talk.

I went inside the bedroom, and it was decked out just as well as the rest of the house. It was almost like this bedroom was already prepared for Me. I checked the closet and drawers of the plushed out bedroom, and there was all type of new clothes and underwear that was exactly my size. I wondered what were chances that Tiger knew my exact sizes. But then again, it was not that hard to tell since I was not that big. Still, I laid out the new clothes to take a shower, and all I could think about was how I was going to be able to clear the situation up back in my neighborhood. Nobody knew for sure that I was the one who killed Nate, but surely I would be suspected of being that we had a lot of beef between the both of Us. I also remembered that I did not change my voice when I kneeled down to Madison to check on her. Now I was becoming nervous and paranoid, realizing that the job I had done was sloppy and not professional.

After getting Myself together, I stepped out into the living room where Tiger and his brother's Pit and Shark were chilling on the couch. They all looked at me with grins on their faces, "Damn, whasup' Killa!? I mean Lil' Mello??? That young Nigga Nate must've really pissed you off, huh? The hoods down there scorching hot right now! we can't even make no money with all the police down there investigating and shit." Pit complained.

"Yea Nate's Brothers is down there trippin' talkin' bout they were close to catching their Brother's Killer, but he got away. You're faster than you look Lil' Mello." Shark said as Hisself and Pit gave each other a play laughing. Not up for the laughs and giggles, I just shook my head and flopped on the couch across from them.

Tiger saw the worried look on my face and asked me if I was okay and what was I thinking about. I told him that I was thinking about what I had just done if anybody suspected me as the killer and if I could've done a better job, then what had just happened. Tiger chuckled as he stood to his feet" Well, you know me, and I'm not gon' bullshit you.. Nate's Brothers fasho are suspecting you, but I will handle that Myself. " Tiger stated.

"What I guess is funny to me is that you just splattered that Niggas brains, your enemies' brains all over the block, and got away with it. Yet, you're not happy with your performance? That's the mindset of a True Killer, and you would only become better now that your realizing what you have done wrong. I will...we will help you become a more Professional Killer so that you would be proud of the jobs you complete. Don't you get it Lil' Mello. This is your true calling Lil' Bro, forreal!" Tiger spoke to me like he was a motivational speaker or something. I sat there hypnotized by Tiger's coaching, and it actually made a lot of sense. As bad as I didn't want to become my father, It seemed like I had already transformed. I've had my first taste of blood, and it graced my taste buds as If I should've been killing for a living.

After killing Nate, I realized that this killing people thing was not as bad as I thought, I had no remorse, nor did I regret what I had done. That's how I knew that I would do it again. I exhaled, "So what do I do about Nate's Brothers and everybody else who think I killed Nate? Do I kill them too? Do I go back to the hood like nothing happened and continue working for Dime?" I asked Tiger.

Tiger and his Brothers chuckled, "Do you kill them too? Nawl Boy, whatchu' gon' do, kill the whole neighborhood? Nawl, I already told you I will...we will handle Nate's brothers, and as far as anybody else who suspects, we use that fear to run shit. If the hood is fearing you, they also respect you, and with respect, we could get almost anything that we want, feel me? As far as working for

Dime, that shit is dead. You know longer work for his Petty Ass, it's time for you to start getting real money, and that's with Us. Anything that you need I could provide it for you, you know longer need the Hood or Dime." Tiger told Me.

I was with everything Tiger was saying, but the leaving the Hood alone part I was not with. I still had my Mother to look after, and when I told Tiger that he told me that either he or his brothers would always take me down there to visit and make sure that she is doing okay. When I heard that, I felt a bit relieved knowing that I was in good hands now. Tiger then told me that the room that I had got dressed in was mine as well as all of the clothes and everything else in that room. Tiger and his brothers stood up giving me play and congratulating me on joining their Team, their family....

I flopped in my new queen-sized bed and stared up at the ceiling, wondering why I had not been joined Tiger's Crew. In the last couple of hours, my life had changed drastically, but I could not yet tell if it was for the better or worse. The good thing about being here was that I had a stable house to live in, I didn't have to provide for anyone, but Myself and I would finally be making real money. The worse part about living here was that there would be stipulations.

Being up under Tiger and his Brother's wings, I would have to do what I been trying to avoid doing, which was killing people for a living. my only question was just how much killing would I have to do? I then began to wonder how long Tiger had been planning for a situation like this to happen. Was it a coincidence that he knew all of my sizes, or had the been plotting? Is that why Tiger been motivating me to kill for him? I had no idea, but one of these days, I would have answers for all of my questions.

I heard two knocks at the door, and Tiger walked right in, "Yo' Lil' Mello, ummm I need the clothes you had on when you took care of that business, and I need the pistol that you used for it." Tiger said with a garbage bag in his hand. I understood that he would get rid of the clothes that Nate's blood had splattered on, but I was not too fond of handing over the pistol my father giving me. I turned my face up, not really wanting too,"Mannn, My Old Man, gave me this pistol man. I can't just give it to..." I was saying before he cut me off. "Look, I understand all of that, but you can't just be out on the streets with the same gun you bodied a nigga with. If the police got a hold of you with the murder weapon you would be finished. Now give it to me so I could get rid of all of these clothes and the pistol so that you could never make the slightest mistake and get it caught up." Tiger told me.

Again Tiger made the most sense but giving up the only gift my father had given me was not easy. I pulled the gun out and stared at it. I was not only staring at it, but I was second-guessing, giving it up because it had a body on it that I murdered. He could easily take it down to the precinct and get me booked, I was sure that would not happen, but it was a possibility. "Lil Mello, don't trip, I'm doing this for you. Trust me, imma' buy you a million more guns that look just like this one." Tiger assured me. I exhaled as I handed it over to him, "Whatchu' gon' do with it?" I asked. Tiger looked me in the face, "I'm getting rid of it so it could never be found again, trust me He said before leaving the bedroom.

Chapter

4

EIGHT YEARS LATER

I stepped outside in the Community College parking lot, that I was attending with my backpack over my shoulder while looking down at my Rolex for the time. I had to rush and get to my old neighborhood by 4 p.m., that was the time my mother normally would come home to ask me for money for a fix. "Hey Romello, me and Latoya were going to grab a bite to eat then go to my house afterward to chill and watch a few movies, wanna' come?" Stephanie asked with a grin on her face. Stephanie and Latoya were some straight cuties that were in a few of my classes. They often invited me to join them after class, but I always had an excuse as to why I couldn't make it. "Ummm, Nawl, not this time, ladies.. I have somewhere to be, but I will take a raincheck if that's okay with yall? I told them with a smile on my face while throwing my backpack into the backseat of my car.

"Mmmm-hmm, you tell us that all the time. We starting to think that you don't find us attractive." Latoya replied. I shook my head, "Nawl, that's not it at all; both of yall are beautiful, but I just am focused on school shit and my money, that's all. Soon doe, I'll accept yall offer real soon. I'll see yall later doe!." I answered before hopping in my car. "We gon' hold you to that!" Stephanie said before they got inside their car.

✳ ✳ ✳

I been living at the same house Tiger allowed me to live in for years now and no matter how long I been here it still never really felt like a home. Tiger swore that he was a father figure, but I looked at him more like an older brother type of male figure in my life. Indeed he did keep his word and provided any and everything that I needed since I been around. Tiger was the one who got me my dodge charger; he got it from one of the white men that he was squeezing out in the suburbs who owned a car dealership. Now don't get it twisted, all the shit Tiger was doing for me did not come for free. In exchange for it, I had to kill anybody that he ordered me to kill. I had become an official hitman, and I was very good at it. I was so good at it Tiger and his brothers were some of the most feared and respected niggas on Detroit's Eastside. They were rich niggas, and it all came from Extorting Hustlers,Business Men, and guaranteeing his protection against any other crew that though they were like them. I could not even lie, I enjoyed the fruits of being a part of Tiger's team because of all the respect and benefits that we were given. It was like we were celebrities. If you were not with us, then you were against us. Most of the time, even when they didn't want to be with us they would join just because it was the safest thing to do...

I pulled up and parked in my driveaway when I looked four houses down and seen Felicia and her cousin Shawna standing in front of *Tabs Spot* dancing and smoking a blunt. Felicia was my girlfriend, and Tab was the neighborhood weed man who kept the hoodrats over his house. When Felicia noticed that I had seen her, she stopped laughing and giggling, knowing that she had fucked up. I had been in a relationship with her for the longest year over, and it seemed like it was only becoming longer. She was stressing me out with all of her rat tendencies, and I often questioned myself why I was with her. The only thing that kept me down my old block, watching just how much things had changed over the years. Nobody that lived in the neighborhood back then when I did still lived neighborhood. The only people that still lived in the area were my deceased arch-enemy Nate's father, and he lived there by himself. I heard that Madison had gone off to college, where I wanted to go, which was Michigan State University. I also heard that her brothers were now street hustlers and sold drugs for the same man I use to work for, Dime. I rode passed their house every day, hoping that one day I would be able to run into Madison, but I never did. I haven't seen her since killing her brother, and ever since then, I wondered how she had been doing. I would often ask Tiger and his brothers if they saw or heard anything about her, and they would always tell me that she was doing better than ever now. I thought about her a million times and had a million "WHAT IF?" questions, but reality always would set in reminding me that it would never happen...

✳ ✳ ✳

I stepped out of my car, grabbing my backpack and heading to the front door when Tab called my name, "Yo' Mello? Mello? Lil' Mello, whasup! You just getting out of school, boy? I remember them days, but them books don't pay the bills doe' homie!" Tab said, laughing. Even Felicia's cousin Shauna laughed at his ignorant comment.

I had to ignore his stupidity; He clearly had no idea that I had money, and if I ever felt for a second that I didn't have enough that I would rob and kill niggas like him to get it. Living in this particular neighborhood, it was best that I kept a low profile. I didn't need to bring any new beef or unwanted attention to the same house that I kept as many guns and weapons as the military and as much money as the banks. I put on a fake grin, "Yea fasho Tab, I hear you." I replied, remaining cool not showing exactly how mad I actually was. One thing that I knew for sure was that Tab didn't want to end up on my "NIGGAS TO KILL "list.

I walked into my house, tossing my car keys and backpack on the kitchen table and I walked over toward the couch where flopped at the long nights and early mornings exhausting. I sat there anxious to leave Detroit and the lifestyle that I was living. The only way that I would be able to leave would be by saving all the money that I was making and to start keeping the extras that I would find. I would go and do a job for Tiger and his brothers, and they would tell me to bring back all of the work and money, but a majority of the time, it would be more there than they would expect. I never would take the extras because I was loyal to the men that were taking care of me over the years, but there have been many times that I was tempted to do so. Five-thousand dollars was starting to not be enough for the people that I would kill, especially the ways that I would do it. I was killing big time high rollers that had a lot of money, but I was steady making the same pay for everyone that I killed.

One time I was bitten by a vicious Pitbull and spent two hours getting stitched up. I was ready for a pay increase next time he needed me I was for sure requesting a pay increase. I only had seventy-five thousand dollars saved up, and my goal before I left the city was two hundred and fifty thousand dollars. I wanted to move to New York and become a writer/journalist since I was such a good writer and storyteller. Two hundred and fifty thousand would be enough for me to live comfortably and start my career.

The doorbell rang, interrupting my deep thoughts and planning, and I already knew who it was. I got up and answered the door letting Felicia in and closing the door behind her. "Hey baby, just getting out of school. "Felicia asked, attempting to kiss me. I dodged her lips and walked passed her on the couch, "Yep, just took my finals, so hopefully, I passed. By next year I plan on being out of here, then you won't have to sneak off and fuck wit' yo' boy Tab." I answered her sarcastically. She smacked her lips sitting inside me, Awww, my baby is mad at me? C'mon, now you know that I wasn't doing nothing over there. We were only over there listening to his new song than he rolled a blunt. That was it." She explained.

Not really trying to hear her pathetic excuse, I just folded my arms but had an ulterior motive in mine. She rubbed the back of my head. "Aww don't be mad at me, boo, you know how I feel about you." She told me, sticking to my plan. I continued acting like I was med. Felicia's hands want from the back of my head to my chest, down to my abs , all the way down to my basketball shorts. "I know what would make you feel better; I got just the thing." She said as she reached down in my shorts.

Felicia pulled my dick out from my shorts, and without hesitation, she stuffed it inside her mouth. She began sucking, licking, and before I know it I was already brick hard and my dick was covered in saliva. Felicia was the truth with her head game; it had to been her one and only talent because I know of nothing else that she had talent in. While she sucked my dick she twisted with both hands on some straight *Superhead* style head. She knew how to please her man, and with the sexy moans that she was making I was sooo turned me on even more. "You still mad at me, baby? Huh? I asked you if you're still mad? She asked, staring up at me with a grin on her face.

When I didn't answer, she went to the spot that would for

sure get me to respond and started licking and sucking on my scrotum sack. "I asked you... If you're still mad at me? answer me!" She asked again. No longer able with my fake attitude and sliding up the couch. "Nawl, Nawl, Nawl, I'm not mad at you no more!" I answered, enjoying the oral services that she was performing.

She then raised her hand up with a smile, knowing that I would tap out, "You betta' not be!" she answered, still holding my brick hard dick in her hand. I then stood up, telling her to turn around and bend that ass over.

I raised the short dress and slid her thong to the site just enough to where I could slide this python inside of her. I licked the tips of four of my fingers and massaged her pussy to prepare her for this big dick that she was gonna soon receive. I snatched my shirt off and stuffed my big-long black hard dick inside of her aggressively how I knew that she liked it. Felicia instantly began to sigh and moan when I started thrusting my dick back and forth inside her pussy.

The sight of her big fat nice ass was certainly motivating me to pound on her pussy harder and harder, demanding that my name be screamed throughout the house. The waves vibrating through her ass was so intriguing that I only wanted the waves to get bigger. I put my hands on both of her shoulders, making sure that I was in control while I gave her the longest strokes. "You like this dick? Do you like this fuckin' dick, girl?" I yelled. Her moans and screams had gotten louder and sounded even sexier, "Ohhhhhh yessss!! I love dis' dick daddy!!" she yelled while throwing that ass back and looking at it while she did it.

"Bitch, don't let me catch you over a...nother...niggasss..house..a fuckin' gain!!!" I yelled back at her in between my hard thrusting and pulling the dick out shooting all of my nut all over her ass. She flopped on the couch onto her stomach, out of breath, and only able to whisper. "Okay, Daddy, Okay, Daddy, I promise. She answered.

Breathing heavy. I pulled my shorts and walked to my back bedroom, flopping on my bed. Felicia walked into my bedroom with a smile of satisfaction on her face as she laid beside me laying her hand on my chest. "Mello? Do you love me?" she asked me. Quickly becoming irritated by her question, "What?! What made you ask me that. I don't... I'm not in the mood for dis' Felicia. I'm trying to get me some sleep before my brothers come through here, so if you gon' stay, then stay, but you gotta be quiet. If not, you could leave!" I told her.

She exhaled, "I'm just saying nigga, you don't treat me like I'm yo' bitch. All we do is fuck, we never go out, and you don't even let me ride with you anywhere, you don't buy me shit...I mean, damn! It's like we not even together!" Felicia said, raising her voice. I turned my head away from hers and closed my eyes, "Well if that's how you feel then It's no point of us being together is it?" I returned a question, still trying to get some sleep. She smacked her lips and, with attitude, slid to the other side of the bed with folded arms. She was right; I didn't include her in anything and never planned on it. Even though we would say that we were in a relationship, it was more like just a sexual relationship. I couldn't take Felicia seriously because she was a bonafide hoodrat that had no intention of changing. She was content with living in the neighborhood and smoking weed for the rest of her life.

Me, on the other hand, had big dreams and goals, and it had nothing to do with the hood or living in Detroit. Truth be told, I was only using her for my sexual purposes, that was the only thing that she was good for. I could never talk to her about my life and my future plans because she wouldn't be able to understand nor feel where I was coming from....

⁇

Chapter

5

10 P.M LATER THAT NIGHT

I was awakened by the loud stereo system that was in the living room, and it only meant that Pit and Shark were here. Even though they all had their own homes out in the suburbs, and their own stash houses, they still would come over and use this house as their *CHILL HOUSE*, I hated it. They would bring their women over all times of the night and trash the place like it was a crack spot. Tiger was the mature one and only came over when it was time to discuss business. He would also come to make sure that I was still on my shit. He had to make sure that his hitman was all the way good. My bedroom door opened when I quickly sat up, signaling for Pit to close the door because I didn't want Felicia to wake up. Not caring about nothing that I was talking about, Pit yelled out, "Oh shit, who is that? Is that my baby girl Felicia? Oh, my bad.Umm Tiger said that he bout' to pull up in a minute and for us to make sure that everybody was gon' so we could talk." Pit said, shutting the door behind him. I was irritated by Pit's ignorance and disrespect. I tapped Felicia's shoulder telling her that it was time to get up and that she had to leave. I walked Felicia to the front door and couldn't help but notice how Pit and Shark were all in my business. They sat on the couches smoking and drinking while staring at Felicia's fat ass, "So are you gonna' call me?" Felicia asked me. I shrugged my shoulders, "I don't know, maybe tomorrow cuz' I'm a lil sleepy." I answered.

Her face turned up, knowing that I was lying, "So tell me now, Mello, are we together or not?!" She asked with her hands on her hips. I looked at her like she was crazy, "Didn't we talk about this already?! No, Felicia, we do not need to be together right now. Now go, we could talk about this tomorrow!" I said, raising my voice and opening the front door for her to leave. Felicia was pissed off and cursed me out while stomping out of the house and down the sidewalk. She called me all type of "BITCH ASS NIGGAS, BROKE ASS NIGGAS, HOE ASS NIGGAS and added a dozen FUCK YOU'S!" showing exactly all of her hoodrat ways. Tiger walked up from the driveway. Damn, whatchu' do to that girl, lil bro?" He asked, stepping into the house. Both Pit and

?

Shark were laughing as I closed the front door behind
Tiger. "Yo Mello, since you don't want her, you should
let me get her. I'll show you how you pose to have that
young thang in check." Pit said to me. I just shook my
head and told him that I didn't care what he did with
her.

Tiger sat down, "Aight yall, I came over here to tell yall
that me going out tonight. We not doing no homework or
laying on nobody tonight, but I want us to show our
faces. We hitting Club Status for Shadow's Welcome
Home Party." Tiger told us. Hearing him say that we
were going to Club Status caught my attention. Shadow
was a real O.G from our old neighborhood who just
came home from doing a ten-year bid, he was also
Dime's older brother. "Yep, so you get to see that bum
ass nigga Dime who you use to work for and with him
being there I know all of his lil workers gone be there
too, R.I.P Nate's brothers." Tiger said to me.

It's been years since I saw Madison's brothers Man-Man
and Stone, in fact, it's been since I killed their brother
Nate. I wasn't worried though, In the eight years since I
saw them a lot had changed. I was a twenty-two-year-
old straight killer now who was in the best shape ever

and was nobody to be played with. Even though Tiger and his brothers cleared my name with anything to do with Nate being killed, I know for sure that they didn't want any problems with me. I just hoped visiting the new club that was in our old neighborhood meant that I would be able to see Madison, who I often thought about. I wanted to see her for years, but as soon as her brother was killed she had moved to her mother's house up in Lansing, Michigan.

"I want you to go get dressed and wear this tonight; I picked it up at one Jewelry Store out in Grosse Pointe that's paying us for protection." He told me, handing me a big diamond roped chain. Amazed at all the diamonds shining and how big it was, I put the chain on and thanked him for the gift he had given me. Pit saw the chain that Tiger got me and instantly started hating asking why would Tiger get me a diamond chain. "Nigga cuz' I wanted too! Buy yo' own fuckin' chain nigga; you got the money! Didn't I just bless you with that new property that brings in at least twenty-thousand dollars a month?! Damn! Stop tricking so much on them hoes, and you could buy yo'self a chain!" Tiger snapped. With Pit being the youngest brother, he was use to being spoiled by Tiger and hated to see me treated like family. Pit was often jealous of how I was treated but all he could do is sit back and shut up about it because Tiger was not trying to hear it. Right, that's what I thought! Yall C'mon, and lets hit this club up. Lil Mello you riding with me." Tiger said, heading toward the front door.

"Why he get to ride wit..."Pit was ready to complain until Tiger quickly turned and gave him a look that said: "I WISH YOU WOULD." Pit decided not to finish his statement. Tiger stepped outside, and I went to get dressed. Witnessing Tiger defend me like I was his actual blood made me feel like family. He wouldn't let anybody fuck with me, and I wouldn't let anybody fuck with him. From the outside looking in, we really looked like we were brothers...

Club Status

6

It was very seldom that we would go to a club and not be on business, so whenever we did, we would do it big and in style. We pulled up to the Club's Valet in Tiger's red BMW745 that was sitting on 24-inch rims, Pit was behind us in his Blue Range Rover Truck that was sitting on 24-inch rims and Shark was behind him in his Orange Jaguar. Everybody hopped out of their foreign cars icy and crispy clean how The Detroit niggas usually did. We all walked straight up to the front of the line giving the bouncers play, walking passed the shakedowns and metal detectors not having to pay the entry fee. We were known but mainly feared, which

☐

allowed us to do whatever we wanted to do. We mobbed through the club heading toward the V.I.P section when Manny, the club owner, stopped in front of us with a nervous grin on his face. ' Hey, Tiger, brother, how you doing? I didn't know yall were coming tonight. You should've called me. Hey Guys, yall looking nice, everybody fine? Everybody good?" Manny was saying as he literally could not stop shaking. Tiger looked down at the out of shape sorry excuse for a man, "Manny what the fuck you mean I should've called you?! I ain't gotta' call you, but only when it's time for me to pick my money up from you once a month. Get the fuck outta my face and make sure there ain't nobody in my booth. Send ten bottles over there too." Tiger told him, trying to walk passed him but was stopped again. "Ummm ten bottles? Okay, I got you..ummm Tiger, I really wish that you would've called me before you came so that way I would've reserved your booth." You see, Dime had already come months ago paying me in advance to make sure that I had everything all set for this Welcome Home Party, and he specifically asked for that booth... Your booth.

Business was slow last month and for me to pay you I had to accept money. I'm so sorry." Manny apologized to Tiger with sweat beads rolling down his forehead. "So you want me and my brothers to sit at the second-best booth is what you're seeing telling me?!" Tiger asked, starting to get mad. Shark stepped up to Manny, "I suggest you figure something the fuck out then because we not sitting nowhere one but at *Our Booth Nigga!*" he said, poking Manny in his forehead aggressively. Before we even sat down a problem was being created, I stood by Tiger, and his brothers began to surround Manny getting ready to fuck him up when Dime. His older brother Shadow and Madison's brothers maneuvered through the coming toward us, "Is that my young dawg Tiger and his crew?! Awww Man,Whasup?! Whasup wit' yall boys?!" Shadow said with a big smile on his face, happy to see all of us. Tiger and his Brothers seen who just approached us, and a smile was even on Tiger's face. Shadow wasn't only like a bigger brother to me but was also like big brother to Tiger.

Back in the day Shadow taught Tiger everything about the streets and taught him how to be the boss that he later in life became. I remember growing up, and every time I saw Shadow, I would see Tiger right beside him. They were tight until Shadow was sentenced to a ten-year prison bid, and there were many rumors roaming around the neighborhood as to what had happened between the two.

The main rumor was that Shadow's girlfriend later heard of all the women that Shadow had while they were together and badly sought revenge. When she saw Tiger, she made it her business to get back at her ex-boyfriend by fucking Tiger. She knew it would get to him and that she could have Tiger whenever she wanted him. She fucked Tiger, developed feelings for him, and showed him where all of Shadow use to hide his work. With Tiger being not happy by how he was being paid by Shadow, he didn't think twice about taking everything that Shadow owned. When Shadow's girlfriend finally noticed that she had been played just like how she tried playing Shadow, she tried fighting Tiger, but there was only so much that she could do.

As time passed by, Shadow's ex-girlfriend had disappeared and never was to be seen again. The rumors were that she killed herself, some said Tigger killed her. The rest of the rumors were that she packed up and moved far away. No one actually knew the truth but Tiger. Another word on the street was that Shadow had called Tiger a million times afterward, but Tiger never answered, leaving the situation still open. "Oh shit, look who we have here... Shadow in the Mothafuckin' flesh, Whasup dawg !?" Tiger said, giving him a play and a man hug. Both crews stared at the other, both Man-Man and Stone took a second look at me like they were shocked to see me. It had been years since the last time we all seen each other, I took a look at the both of them noticing how they both had on a little jewelry, but I could tell they did not see any real money. They were both working for the same people that I use to work for back when I was younger, and I was sure that they were getting bird fed how I use to.

So what's going on here, my man Manny causing yall problems or something? "Shadow asked, putting his arm around Manny's shoulder. Tiger grinned. "Nawl, there ain't no problem here, ain't that right, Manny? Ole' Manny here was just telling us how he was about to move yall crew outta' our booth and into another one because he made a mistake in allowing yall to sit there." Tiger answered, staring into Manny's face. Manny began to try and explain himself, but Shadow cut him off, "Hmmm, so Manny.You took my Lil' brothers' money that he paid you for that particular booth, and you already had it reserved for them? Manny, Manny, Manny... Aight, just give us the money back, and we could go to the second booth across the room." Shadow told Manny.

Scared to death, Manny told Shadow he didn't have the money because he included it in the monthly payment that he paid to Tiger. There was a brief moment of silence. "Well you know what? Don't nobody trip...We gon' take the other booth tonight and everybody will be happy, Aight? Okay? Tiger, you and your crew, take the booth, and have a good night." Shadow told us. What the fuck?! What about my fuckin' money?" Dime was asking and ready to trip until Shadow gave him a type of look. I could tell that Tiger was a bit surprised at how willingly Shadow agreed to sit somewhere else. Shadow knew that Tiger was the man in the hood and therefore he respected it for the time being. Both crews began walking our separate ways when we heard Man-Man say, bitch-ass nigga. Under his breath.

Quickly Pit and Shark turned around. "Whatchu' say nigga?! What the fuck did you just say?! Say it again! They both yelled, trying to get over to both Man-Man and Stone. The bouncers moved in quickly, making sure that nothing happened between both parties. We all went our separate ways with mugs on all of our faces; they hated us just as much as we hated them.

When we made it to our booth, both Pit and Shark were

?

still pissed off that they were not able to handle Shadow and his crew. Surprisingly Tiger was not as mad as his brothers. Instead, he was weirdly calm. Shark noticed how calm Tiger was when he had to ask him why. Tiger had a face that read he was deep into his thoughts, "Hmmm, Shadow voluntarily gave us the booth they already paid for..Why?" He asked himself. Pit and Shark had no idea, but I was far from stupid and knew that it was deeper than it appeared.

"That Nigga is on some sneaky shit Tiger, I feel it." I told him. Tiger nodded his head, "Yea I know, but what is he on?" Tiger asked. "If I was him, I would figure out a way to kill you or have you killed," I answered. Pit and Shark both told me to shut up, but Tiger told them to both shut up. "He's right. Your right, I would wanna' kill me too if I was him...well I got something for his ass, he won't even see it coming. I want you to keep an eye on him Lil' Mello, we not gon 'kill him tonight, but it is in his future. Have fun tonight fellas and wait for any potential jobs." Tiger told us, handing all of us a bottle that the waitress had just bought to our booth.

Tiger and I sat in the booth observing everyone else enjoy themselves, including Pit and Shark, who were out on the dance floor freakin' the ladies. I never was the club type of guy, nor did I smoke or drink, so I didn't mind sitting in the back watching everyone else. Tiger gulped from his bottle when the waitress came to our booth with four bottles of champagne. " This is from Shadow and his crew over there, enjoy." she said before dropping them off with a small note on the side.

Tiger picked up a bottle and the small note reading it, after he finished he let out a light chuckle. Holding the bottle up he acknowledged that he received it. I asked what did that note say and he kept a smile staring over looking at Shadow and to crew. "Yea, he gotta' go. I want you to kill him, all of them." He said in a low tone.

I mobbed through the clubs' crowded dance floor into the restroom to take a piss, and it just so happened that Mann-Mann, Stone and Shadow were all inside as well. They were all huddled up talking until they saw me, I looked them all in their faces as I headed to the urinals.

"Hmmmm,look who it is we got here..Lil Mello done grew up, even gotta lil size to him. Got his lil' chain on, watch getting money now, huh since you been wit Tiger huh?"Stone asked as he took a look at me. "Yes it's been, haven't seen him in years since me, you and Nate whooped his ass," Man-Man said than laughing.

I grinned as I walked over to the sink to wash my hands, "Yes it's been a while, looks like one of yall missing. Maybe yall done jumped on the wrong nigga." I replied sarcastically. Offended by my slick comment, Man-Man walked toward me like he wanted to do something, but Shadow stepped in between us, telling him to relax. I stared all three of them down,

"So Lil' Mello... Damn, time flies by. I remember when you were a young nigga breaking in people's cars and houses stealing shit now, you all grown up. You all in shape in shit like you were the one that was in the gym. Well, I guess you out here working for Tiger now huh?"

⏃

Shadow asked as he stepped back, taking a look at me. I ignored his question, "So.... ten years in the joint..huh? Now what you gon' do?" I asked.

"Imma take what's mine in due time. Starting with the hood then the city." He answered.

I chuckled " Betta' be careful, It's gon' be hard to take."I replied.

"Thanks for the tip but let me ask you something. What position do you think you play in Tiger's organization? Shadow asked. Without hesitation I answered that the position I played was a family member. When Shadow heard family members, he began to laugh, "Family?! Are you serious?! family?! Dat' nigga wouldn't know what family is if it slapped him in the face. Now I know Tiger and I know that he is using you as one of his pawns. The question is, how long will you allow him to use you as his pawn before you make the power move? I'm telling you young dog, the minute you began to venture off and want to do your own thing is the moment that he would show you his true colors. You watch what I tell you." Shadow said, giving his crew the head nod to follow him out.

Before leaving out of the restroom, Shadow turned around, giving me one last look, "Look Lil' Mello, Tiger may be treating you like family now, but he would never treat you like he treat his brothers. Think about it, did he give you any of his properties? You got a big house out in the suburbs as they do? I only seen three foreign cars out there, and I'm willing to bet you that none of them are yours." Shadow said, leaving the restroom and leaving me standing there thinking about all of what he just said. I turned around taking a look at myself in the mirror; I had to find out if Tiger really considered me as family....

Homework/Execute

7

Tiger and I were headed to another club, but this time we were all about business. Tiger was telling me that Manny, the Club Owner that we had paid for protection, had put us up on a baller nigga that he knew that was spending and would be an easy hit for us. Not only were we going to get this baller nigga for everything that he had, but I also had to find out if what Shadow was telling me about Tiger was true. I decided to start by telling him that I wanted a pay increase on the jobs that I been completing so I could pay for the extra college courses that I planned on taking. I also told him that every mission was becoming more and more dangerous. Tiger tried convincing me that five-thousand dollars were the going rate to have somebody killed. He also added all of the losses that he been taking lately, so at the moment, he couldn't raise my pay but promised in the future that he would. He even went as far as to tell me that the house that I was living in for the past few years had become one of his biggest bills with the constant repairs and damages that he had to get fixed.

Right then, I knew that the conversation was not getting anywhere, and I knew then that if I wanted a pay increase that I would have to start pocketing things from all of my victim's homes. "Another thing that I needed to talk to you about is how your brothers be coming through not considerate at all of the company I have. Them niggas is trifling, and all they do is trash that bitch like it's a Trap House or something. They don't give a fuck that I live there, man." I complained to Tiger. Tiger laughed, "Aight man, I'll holla' at them." He replied. I had a feeling that Tiger was not taking anything that I just discussed to him about as an serious issue, and that would soon be a problem....

We sat in the VIP section on straight chill mode, watching the young niggas standing by the stage clowning and throwing their money at the strippers. There were a lot of people standing by the stage, but there was one particular crew that we could tell were all together. There were at least ten of them. These ten niggas were showing mad love to all of the strippers and waitresses, and they all were fresh to death while they did it. These young niggas were shining wearing all of their jewelry and all of that, but there was a fat Nigga that was sitting in the booth behind them that was wearing all of the iciest jewels. He had racks of money on the table in front of him; it was not a secret that he was the real big nigga of the crew.

That gotta be him right there, Tiger, the fat one in the booth wearing all of the jewelry. I told Tiger, he squinted his eyes, "Yea it gotta be, but I'm waiting on Manny's Homeboy Paco to step out and signal that he is the one fasho'. If not, we would get him too." Tiger told me. I couldn't complain too much about the waiting because how could I when there was naked and half-naked women that were dancing and constantly walking by us.

Plus there was a group of women across from us that were having themselves a Bachelorette Party tonight, so it really didn't bother me just to wait around. Tiger was totally focused on our agenda in being here tonight. He wouldn't drink or smoke and had become irritated in waiting on Manny's friend. He told me to go to the bar and order for Paco and then to come out.

I stood at the crowded bar and asked the bartender to go and get Paco for me while I waited. A soft hand rubbed the back of my head when I quickly turned around, and a stripper stepped in between my legs, "Hey, Cutie, I know you want a dance." She said in her sexy tone. I looked the stripper up and down and couldn't help but to stare at her tattooed fat-ass, "Ummm, damn baby. No, thank you, not right now." I answered her. She just smiled and gave me a sexy look and told me that she would be back a bit later. I turned back toward the bar and exhaled at the restraint it took to deny the stripper. The bartender then told me that Paco would be out shortly. I stood at the bar patiently waiting for Paco when I heard a familiar voice standing behind me, telling her friend that was beside me that she doesn't drink.

Curious as to who it was that voice belonged to, I turned around and my face damn near fall down to the counter. "Ma... Madison?! Is that you? I asked. She looked at me, "Romello?! Wha.. what are you...I mean how are you?" She asked with a smile. The smile on my face grew bigger.

"I'm good. I'm good. How are you? Whatchu' doing

here?" I answered and returned the question. "I'm good, um...one of my sorority sisters is getting married tomorrow, so I'm here celebrating with her and the rest of our sorority sisters," Madison answered.

I took a look at her, and she was more beautiful then I remembered. Redbone skin, long red hair that was all hers, a small petite body, nice sized breast, a plump-ass, and she looked good as hell. I was damn near speechless, "Well come here, girl and give me a hug; I haven't seen you in what? Seven or eight years?!" I told her opening my arms for a hug. We hugged each other tightly.

"WOW!! It's good to see you, like what are you doing here? You never seemed like the type of guy that would come here for a good time." Madison asked me. I looked around the club then back to her. "Yea, I'm not. I'm actually here with Tiger. He got me here with him visiting a few of his dancer friends." I answered. Madison's friend loudly cleared her voice, interrupting our conversation, introducing herself as her best friend and sorority sister Ebony. We shook hands, "Well, I hate to interrupt yall reunion, but we gotta' got back over to the Bachelorette over there sooo.." Ebony was saying, Pablo, the owner of the club, finally stepped out from the back. "Oh, hey, you must be Manny's peoples. Ummm, well there..." Pablo was saying before I cut him off. Madison and her best friend Ebony were ready to head back over to their section when I stopped them, "Hey Madison, ummm, you should let me call you so we could do lunch or something." I suggested.

She grinned, "Yes, I'd like that, call ,me." She told me, followed by her number. We told each other to have a good night, and both went our separate ways. I finished talking to Paco and went back to our V.I.P booth. After my talk with Paco, I told Tiger that the guy that we suspected was exactly who it was. It was time for our meet and greet. We both headed over into their section and straight toward the Fat boss nigga. "Whatup doe' Big boy, enjoying yourself?" Tiger asked with a sneaky and devilish grin on his face. Surrounded by strippers shaking and clapping their asses, one of these young niggas who I guess had to be his security by how close he was to the fat nigga. Stepping closer toward him, I responded. "Hell yea, good looking. I want you to get us ten more bottles ASAP!" he told us tossing a roll of money into Tiger's hand thinking that we must've worked for the Club. Tiger chuckled and pocketed the bundle of money. "I think you may be slightly confused, big fella, we don't work here. We actually came over here to talk business with you."

Tiger told him. The fat boss nigga told Tiger with the straight face, "Oh I'm not here to talk business; you gotta get wit' me on the weekdays. I'm chilling with my young dogs tonight." He replied.

Getting tired of the fat nigga steady trying to dismiss him I cleared my throat and said, "Again, I say, you must be confused in who you are talking to, and I say that now is the perfect time we discuss business." Tiger said, stepping into their V.I.P booth picking up one of their bottles and pouring himself a drink. The small guy who must have been the security didn't like how comfortable Tiger was making himself and he tried to snatch the bottle out of Tiger's hand but not before blessed him with a hard-left jab to the face that sent him to the floor. The little guy who I sent to the floor fall into a deep sleep and all of them stood still staring at the both of us. We now had everyone's attention, including the fat boss nigga. The fat boss nigga told the strippers to leave his section and asked his young niggas to stand down. I stood in front of the booth securing Tiger, making sure that no one could get close if they tried. I had my hand on my pistol standing guard like I usually did while Tiger discussed the business part of our trip. I stood by while they talked, and I couldn't help but to laugh on the inside on how professional Tiger would be when he was telling crews that he was from that point on extorting them. He would tell whoever we were about to squeeze that we knew all of their business, what they did for a living, then he would tell them the percentage of what he would be taking from them monthly.

At the beginning of every meeting, whoever we were extorting would play the tough role as if they were not going to pay, but after a few minutes of talking to Tiger O.G, they would give in to Tigers promising threats. Tiger was an articulate, professional, and persuasive businessman. He would make the people that he was extorting feel like they badly needed their services and him by their side. One thing that was for sure was that he surely held his and of the that guaranteed protection for everybody that paid monthly. Tiger should have been a lawyer or some type of counselor how he could get into the people's head. I continued standing post securing Tiger's safety while he discussed business with the fat boss Nigga, but I could not stop thinking about my run-in with Madison. I stopped a bypassing waitress and told her to take Madison's section ten bottles of Rosa' from me and to put it on my tab. I stood there watching all of the battles being taken over there, and they were all shocked when they received them. I could tell by their body language that the sorority sisters were asking where did the bottles come from when I saw the waitress pointing over in my direction. They all waved, smiled, and began whispering to Madison like we were teenagers. "Yo, Yo nigga! Let's go, we outta' here. "Tiger told me, putting me on the back.

Before we made it to the front door Madison and two other attractive women approached us; one of them was wearing her wedding veil. "Romello, is it? Hi, I just wanted to thank you for sending over them bottles. That was very sweet of you." The bride to be told me. I nodded my head with a smile, "Awww no problem, your welcome, and congratulations on the wedding." I told her. "Lil' Madison? Is that you?! Whasup girl, you looking good and all grown up. Come over here and give me a hug!" Tiger told her seeing her for the first time.

Madison smiled. "Hi Tiger, thank you, and you're looking good too." she complimented him back. "Soooo... You're getting married, and Lil' Mello here sent over some bottles, huh? That's whasup. He learned from the best." Tiger said , looking over at me with a grin on his face as if he was proud. "Well, ladies, I wish that we could stay and celebrate with yall, but we gotta get up outta here, Madison, It's always good to see you, and I will be calling you. congrats again on your wedding, what's your name again?" I asked. Her friend told me that her name was Sherry, and I hugged all three of them before we handed out of the club.

On the car ride back to the house, I asked Tiger how did the meet and greet go with the fat boss nigga. He told me that it wants how it was supposed to and that he would be getting paid forty-thousand dollars a month, and he would be paying on the seventh. I just nodded my head not surprised by his persuasive tactics. He began telling me that this nigga operated not far from where I lived, but my mind was in a completely different place, and he noticed it. "Yo' Lil' Mello, whassup wit' you? It's like your distracted or something, is this about your run into Madison?" He asked. "Nawl, man, hell nawl... I hear you; he lives not far from where I live." I answered. Tiger looked over at me, "Hey, imma' need you to stay focused and concentrate on getting this money don't let no pussy distract you Lil' Mello, I mean...It's good you bumped into yo' lil friend and all but... "He was saying until I cut him off.

"I'm straight Tiger... I gotchu' I told him. Tiger nodded his head, "Aight man, I hear you." He replied.

Tiger didn't give a fuck about anything other than his money, and business had to act like that was all that I cared about to keep him quiet...

Little Bit 2 Late

8

I was sitting in the kitchen filling out college applications and checking out apartments and condos in the area of the colleges that I was applying for when I saw Tiger pulling into the driveway with all of his brothers in the car with him. I closed my folders up just before Tiger, and his brothers uninvitingly welcomed themselves in, "Whasup Lil' Mello. Whatchu' was in dis bitch doing?" Pit asked, sitting beside me while his other brother flopped on the couch, and Tiger leaned against the wall.

"Shit really, just filling out college applications trying to get in Michigan State hopefully," I answered.

Pit laughed, "Yea, right, you not getting into no good college like that fool them white folks don't want no niggas from the hood at their schools!" Pit said, reaching over grabbing the folder that held all of my applications and apartment and condo books in. I snatched it back from him. "no, them white folks don't want a stupid nigga like you in their schools. At least I'm smart enough to want to do something that could take me out of the hood. " I told him making the both of his brothers laugh at my slick comment.

Anyway, fuck all of that he talking. What got yall riding round together today?" I asked them.

"We just riding around collecting from all of the people that owe up. Ummm, tonight I need you to suit up, though. You remember that young nigga over there on East Warren that runs that spot and drives the Old School on 26's? "

"Yea, that young nigga been dodging all of us for the past three months and now his time is up!" Tiger told me.

"And I hear the young nigga is copping from them niggas that's over there off the freeway too," Shark added.

"Okay, so when does this need to be done? Does he have

a crew that I need to watch out for? What about surveillance or dogs? The last job had to get twenty stitches because they had some crazy-ass pit-bull." I asked.

"This job needs to be done tonight; he has a couple of homeboys but nothing for you to worry about. He don't have any dogs, but he does have cameras all over the place. Tonight he is throwing a party, so that would be a perfect time to catch him slipping. Are you good at your artillery? The gun connect will be here this week with all new shit." Tiger asked. I nodded my head, "Yes, I'm good for now, but I will need all new shit after I pull this one off." I answered him. Tiger said okay, and all of them gave me play before they left the house.

It was only 6 p.m., so I had more than enough time to prepare for my upcoming mission. I walked through the house, through the back door, and into the garage. I moved the tool stand, and under it was where I stashed all of my weapons of mass destruction. I had everything that would allow me to complete a mission without being noticed, such as wigs, costumes, masks, and even makeup. I was a hitman, and one thing that I learned about killing people was that it was best if I didn't look the same as I did when I killed the last victim. I was serious about how I handled my missions, and if I didn't want to be identified, then this was the best way to go about it.

I grabbed two pistols, silencer, two knives, and my wig

that had the braids hanging down. I also bought my AR-15 assault rifle in case shit got real, and I ended up in a big shoot out. No matter what type of job that I had. I made sure that I was always prepared for anything...

(MIDNIGHT)

I pulled up two blocks away from where the job was to and put on my wig and my Detroit fitted cap on top of it. I checked and tucked my pistols into my waistband, put my knives in my pockets and socks, and began walking down the street. The house was already jumping, and music pounding loudly throughout the neighborhood. There was all types of traffic walking in and outside of the house, which was the perfect time for me to slide in. As I got a bit closer, I noticed that it was not as easy as I thought, sitting on the porch was five young niggas and a choppa sitting beside them. They were clearly patrolling the house for any unwanted guest. It was easy to read these young niggas though, all I had to do was sit back and wait on a girl with a fat ass to walk in, and then they would quickly be distracted by that which would give me the time to sneak in while they were not looking.

Making my way through the house I bobbed my head to the music and picked up a Corona bottle pouring half of it out as if I been drinking it while cruising through. I flopped on the couch to observe the layout of the house when I saw a group of girls come in. I recognized one of them, but I couldn't remember where from and I couldn't remember a name. Some girls that were sitting on the couch across from me began screaming when they seen their friends enter the party. "Ebony !! Hey girl!?! I'm so glad you came that nigga Trey been asking for us all night! You look cute though, you ready to get this money?" She asked Ebony. "Hell, yes, girl. Let's get it. Where is Trey by the way?" Ebony asked.

I sat there on the couch pump-faking like I was enjoying the music being played and feeling the beer I was fake drinking, "He's upstairs in the bedroom getting ready for us right now, so come on!" The girl told Ebony while grabbing her hand, pulling her up the stairs with her. On their way up, Ebony and I locked eyes as if we both recognized each other. Right at that moment, I remembered where I knew her from. Ebony was Madison's friend that she introduced me to at the Titty Bar, where they were celebrating their friend getting married. Ebony was the girl that was trying to get Madison drunk at that same bar. Ebony and her friend continued to head up the stairs, she looked like she wanted to say something to me, but I was sure that it was the braids that were throwing her off.

I needed to get up the stairs because of the nigga that they were going to see was the same nigga that I was paying this visit too. Just when I was about to shoot my shot and try and head up the stairs, a female came and fell right into my lap, smelling like nothing but Tequila.

?

"Oh I'm so sorry, excuse me. Imma' bit tipsy and clumsy right now." She said throwing her arm around me. She was actually very attractive, but I had no time for any conversation. "It's... It's fine Sweetheart. Trust me; It's okay. It's not every day that a pretty female just falls into my lap." I complimented her while helping her up. Right then, Trey's homeboys that were once patrolling the porch all came inside the house and chilled on the stairs that led to where Tray was and where I was trying to get. "So, what's your name, cutie?" The drunk girl asked me before sitting beside me. A few of Trey's homeboys walked into the living room, and the only way for me not to be singled out was to use the drunk girl as a distraction in order for me to fit in. "My name is Noella, what's yours?" I returned the question now putting my arm around her shoulder. She told me that her name was Anita and she asked me who was it that I knew at this party. I told her that I knew Trey and now her, she just laughed at my answer, calling me funny. Anita began talking and rambling as she sat beside me, but I was sitting back, plotting on how I would get up the stairs. Trey's homeboys were on guard, but like before, they were easily distracted by any female with a fats ass and some titties.

A couple of his homeboys went into the kitchen where there was some female challenging each other to take some shots of liquor. I figured this was the best time for me to shoot my shot and get up the stairs. I excused myself from Anita, telling her that I had to use the restroom, and I headed straight up the unguarded stairway; "Yo..Yo..where the the hell you think you're going?" One of his homeboys stopped me as he made his way back from the kitchen to asked me.

Being quick on my fast, "Shid, my stomach is fucked up from the wings over there on the table; I was just heading to the bathroom." I answered. The homeboy that stopped me was ugly black nigga who stepped to me with a mug on his face, "There are toilets down here, use them," he told me. I looked around, with all of these people down here. All the bad bitches down here? You don't want me to blow it up cuz' It's gon make everybody leave and nobody gon' gets no pussy. I told him. He looked around knowing that I was making a good point. He looked around knowing that I was making a good point. He looked back at me up and down, "Who the fuck are you anyway Cuz'? I don't remember letting you in and I don't even know you? Who Invited you?" The ugly black nigga asked me.

I stood there trying to get my answers together but wasn't fast enough for him, and that's when he called his mans to come over to us. Pissed that he was called away from the girls they had in the kitchen, he walked over. "Whasup? what the fuck do you want I got these hoes in there bout to get lose?"

His mans asked. The ugly black nigga asked him if he had known me or let me into the party. The guy looked me up and down. "Nawl I don't know that nigga, is that what you called me in here for?" he asked. Noticing that a problem was soon to occur, I braced myself to pull out my pistol if needed. "Look, I know Trey, and that's who told me to come and enjoy myself at his party. Shid, all the money that I be spending with that nigga, it's bout' time that he invited me over to party with him." I said, still holding my stomach like I had to really take a shit. "There it is then; he's a customer so relax." The homeboy told the black nigga.

"Jason, leave my boo alone, damn! He's cool wit.'

Trey, so leave him alone wit' yo' ugly ass!" Anita said, stumbling toward us. Both Anita and homeboy told the ugly black nigga Jason to chill out. Jason looked me in the face skeptical about me and told me to go ahead up the stairs and not to get lost. Anita went back into the living room, and the homeboy went back into the kitchen to the group of females that were in there. When I made it up the stairs, it was a bit more mellow then it was downstairs, I heard females giggling and what sounded like noses snorting. I quietly crept past the bedrooms looking for were the giggles and snorting were coming from when I stopped at the bathroom door. Trey, Ebony, and the other girl were all inside snorting cocaine. While peeking inside, I saw Ebony unbuckling Trey's belt to his pants when he told her to be patient until they made it back to the bathroom, where he wanted to fuck the both of them right. I quietly crept back to the bedroom and was confused as to which one could've been Trey's. I had no idea between the three bedrooms, which one may have been his, and my time was very limited. "Aight ladies, time to take the party to my bedroom. Follow me if yall want some more..right this way," Tray told them. I looked at all three bedrooms when I saw a AK-47 sticking out from under the bad. This had to be his bedroom. I ran right inside the bedroom and hid Inside the closet closing the door behind me.

Trey and both girls walked into the bedroom, closing the door behind them when the girls jumped right in the bed. I pulled my pistol out and attached the silencer to it and waited for the perfect time to proceed with my mission I could've just come right out, killing all three of them, but I already didn't like killing people, so I really tried not to kill anybody that I wasn't ordered to kill if I could. "So let me get this straight, you're willing to pay us five hundred dollars a piece for a threesome?" Ebony asked. A lighter was sparked, and through the closet doors, I could see Trey pulling from his blunt. Thankful for the type of closet door he had, I could see them but couldn't be seen.

"But not just any threesome, the best threesome, I'm talking pussy licking, mad dick-sucking, one girl riding my face while the other girl is riding my dick. That's the type of threesome I'm paying for!" Trey told them. Hearing Trey's threesome request being negotiated, I couldn't help but to get aroused myself. Ebony and her friend were very attractive and super thick. I couldn't wait until this sexual activity happened. I was a bit surprised that a friend of Madison was tricking for money, but I guess the MSU Tuition was more expensive than I thought. "Well, Tiny... You heard what

⁇

the man said, you betta eat this pussy good girl!" Ebony told her friend with a grin on her face while taking off her clothes, "You know I always eat your pussy good anyway!" Tiny replied, also removing her clothes. In a matter of seconds, both girls were in the bed naked and ready for action while Trey sat back ready to watch before My eyes grew back, observing how Ebony had the fattest ass and big titties. Tiny had a nice plumped ass but still a flawless body. She was tattooed up and down her thighs and around her waist that was sexy as hell. They both started off by slowly and passionately kissing each other before Tiny started kissing down Ebony's body down to her pussy. As Ebony laid flat down on her back, enjoying the oral pleasures of Tiny's tongue, she began to moan loudly, and the screams aroused both Trey and me. From where I was standing, Tiny was bent over on all fours with her back so arched that I could damn near see the whole inside of her pussy. After only a few minutes, they switched over to the "69" position, which was the sexiest. Now Tiny laid flat on her back with Ebony's fat ass sitting on her face and pussy on top of her mouth. Ebony, on the other hand, was headfirst into the pussy, both licking and munching on it as if it was her last meal. This indeed was the sexiest girl on girl action I have ever seen.

Having already seen enough, Trey stood up and began taking off his clothes, revealing the erection that he now had. He smacked Ebony on the ass, indicating that it was time for her to raise her face up from Tiny's pussy just enough for her to suck his dick. Now Ebony was riding Tiny's face while sucking on Trey's dick all at the same time. I stood behind the closet door with the hardest dick and badly wanting to join. Ebony was looking like the truth as she sucked Trey's dick, a true Karrine Stephens, with her head game. Trey couldn't even keep still without losing his balance; it wasn't long before Trey couldn't take anymore and needed for everyone to change positions. He then laid flat on his back and requesting for the both of them to suck his dick at the same time. Both Ebony and Tiny started licking and sucking on Trey's dick in the sexiest way. In between times, they both would stop and kiss each other.

With their wet and sloppy tongue kissing, they would let their saliva drip down on his dick so they could continue to suck on him until he was dry. They changed positions again, now with Trey still laying flat on his back. Ebony was riding his face from the back while Tiny was riding his dick. With them both sitting up, it was easy for Ebony to suck on Tiny's titties while getting her pussy ate. "Yea, yea, yea... Mmm shit!!" Ebony screamed in the sexiest tone. Tray tapped on her ass, indicating for her to raise up off his face which was covered with pussy juices. He told Tiny to get on all fours so he could hit her from the back while he ate Ebony's pussy at the same time. After getting in the positions Trey wasted no time in ramming Tiny's pussy from the back.

He placed both hands on each of her shoulders and was straight drilling Tiny making her scream for more and more. Ebony was enjoying her pussy being eaten but felt like she was being robbed because Trey was pounding

Tiny's pussy and not hers. Ebony got up ordering new positions, she wanted to get fucked and was going to make sure that she did. Ebony than laid flat on her back, wanting to be fucked missionary but also wanted pussy to be sat on her face. When they switched positions, Tiny's screams became louder, and Trey was gunning Ebony with aggression. After a few strokes Trey couldn't even take any more. "I'm bout' to bust! I'm bout' to bust!" He moaned out. Ebony smacked Tiny's ass for her to raise up, and both Ebony and Tiny sat on all fours like puppies waiting to be fed a treat with their tongues out. Trey then released and erupted all over both of their faces causing him to flop over on the bed from the exhaustion. Ebony and Tiny's faces were covered in his cum when they faced each other and began to tongue kiss the other and lick each other faces dry of Trey's cum.

All of their highs had come down, and they all cuddled in the bed until they all fell asleep together. I had to give respect where it was given; he fucked the hell out of both the girls. Shid, I would've paid five hundred dollars a piece for them too.

(7.M)

The sun rays beamed into the bedroom down into Ebony's face slowly awakening her. Still standing tall and militant, I watched all of them sleep knowing that the right time to kill Trey would present itself. The ring tone on one of the females' purses went off and woke all three of them up. "Shit! I have an 8 o'clock class; I gotta' go! Hey,wake up! I need that five hundred dollars!"

Ebony nudged Trey getting up to get herself together. She ran into the bathroom ass naked in a rush to leave. Tiny got up, checking her phone saying she had to go too, she also began to get dressed. Trey was up now as well. He picked up his pants from the floor and pulled out a bundle of money, counting out a thousand dollars.

Ebony came back into the bedroom in a rush to grab her stuff and money so she could get out of there. She stood in the mirror, fixing her hair and complaining how late she was going to be. Trey, on the other hand, was sitting there, holding his head in the palm of his hands, probably feeling the effects of a hangover. He reached in his nightstand, pulling out what looked like an ounce of cocaine, stuck his pinky finger inside of it, and took a big snort of it. Tiny seen that went over towards him to get herself a hit. When Ebony seen both of them getting high, she just shook her head before picking up the money that sat on the bed and telling them that she would see them later.

Ebony was so discombobulated that she left one of her fallen earrings on the floor. Tiny asked Trey if he was hungry, and after he answered yes, she told him that she would be in the kitchen cooking them breakfast. Finally, Trey was left by himself, and this was my chance to do what I was here for. Trey walked around the bedroom, ass naked, looking for his boxers that were directly in front of the closet door that I had been hiding behind all night. When he reached down to pick them up, I kicked the closet door open against his head, sending him back to the bed. I had a pistol pointed directly in his face and a finger over my lip, signaling for him to remain silent.

Noticing the big pistol on my hand that had a silencer on it, he followed my directions. I walked over to close the bedroom door to prevent any unwanted guests from entering. "Who the fuck are you?! How'd you get in my fuckin' house?! How'd you get in my fuckin' closet?!" Trey asked me holding his injured head. I slapped my gun across his face hard as hell, "I'm the only one talking right now ! Not you! Now... You owe Tiger some money, and I'm here to kill you since you can't pay yo' street tabs that you owe Tiger. I just might be able to do you a favor if you were to pay me right now!" I told him. As tough as Trey thought he was, he knew that being tough with a pistol in his face wouldn't get him anywhere, so he did what he was supposed to do. He began telling me where everything was from all of his money, his two-hundred thousand dollars' worth of jewelry, and the four bricks of heroin that he had under his bed.

I loaded all of the things I was taking from Trey in one of his Gucci carryon bags and threw it over my shoulder. He then asked me if I was really going to spare him his life, "You see, I never told you that I was going to spare your life. What I told you was that I was going to do you a favor, and that could have meant anything from letting you have an open casket or killing you faster than normal." I said as I raised the pistol back at his face. "You bitch-ass, slime-ball ass nigga! fuck you and fuck Tiger too! My nigga Jason is gon' kill all yall

Niggas..." Trey was saying before I cut him off by sending a bullet through his brains and watching his body fall to the floor. The bedroom door opened, "I forgot my... "Ebony was saying until she seen Trey's body laying beside his splattered brain.

She was in a shock seeing what I guess was her first dead body, but I was shocked to see her walk right in after I did what I had done. Ebony looked up at me and seen me standing there with my pistol in hand when she quickly took off running. I then chased after her down the stairs as she screamed throughout the entire house trying to get away. When Ebony ran through the kitchen, she screamed for Tiny to run before she burst through the side door. After killing Trey I couldn't take the risk in leaving any witnesses, I shot three more shots into Tiny's stomach, causing her to fall on the kitchens floor. I then ran out the side door in an attempt to catch Ebony, but it was already too late, she was pulling off fast and punching her car to the limit down the block.

I stood in Trey's Driveway when I saw all the same niggas that were patrolling the front door and stairs at the party last night. Even the ugly black nigga was standing with all of them to doors down from where I stood.

"Yo, yo, yo aint that the nigga...Why he gotta' gun in his hand?! We gotta holla at that nigga!!" was all that I heard the crew saying to each other. Without hesitation, I raised my pistol at them and began shooting at the entire crew. They all started ducking for cover, but not before I saw that I hit the ugly black nigga Jason in the neck. I took off running down the block with the Gucci bag still on my shoulder when I heard them chasing behind me. Not long before I made it to my car, the crew began shooting at me as well, which made me try and get away quicker. I finally made it to my car, and when I hopped in, I drove backward in attempts to avoid the incoming bullets that were directed for me. Bullets began ripping through my windshield and into my engine, which would only allow me to get so far away. I had to move and move fast while doing it.

When I got far enough down the block, I whipped the car around facing forward to make an even faster getaway and sped away. "Damn! Damn! Damn!" I yelled, pulling away from the scene and slamming on the steering wheel. I was pissed how crazy things had just gotten back at the house; I hated I had to kill Tiny, and I hated that Ebony had got away from me, which left a witness that could possibly testify if she wanted too. I was use to doing clean murders but this one was sloppy and not my best work

I'm Straight
Regardless

9

Four Days Later

I was sitting outside of my nigga Killa Kam's house, waiting for him to bring out the money he was using to buy all of the stuff that I took from Trey's house. I was giving him the sweetest deal that he could not refuse. Four bricks of heroin that price ranged from eighty to a hundred thousand dollars in Detroit. I told him only to give me two hundred and fifty thousand dollars for it.

For the jewelry collection that was worth two hundred thousand dollars, I told Killa Kam to only give me a hundred thousand dollars for it. The majority of the jewelry was customized, but my nigga Killa Kam was a straight hustler that was working with a few million, so I knew he would find something to do with it. Killa Kam had been my nigga since back in high school, and even back then we were much alike. While the other niggas our age were chasing the girls around and sharing clothes with one another, we always were staying to ourselves on separate sides of the classroom.

We both knew that the other was getting money because we were the only two who weren't driving our parents' cars or had Hoopties. We were riding in the latest car that came out the year it was, and we just moved differently than the kids our age. Once we peeped the game of others, we became cool, and later on, down the line, we became friends. Killa Kam was a bit more fortunate then I was, he had his Uncles who lived out in Arizona for that. His Uncles showed him the game, and from that point on, he refused to be nothing less than a millionaire. Killa Kam was my friend and the one and only person I trusted with my life. Killa Kam hopped in my car out of breath from running back and forth when he handed me a brown paper bag. "Whew shit! There you go, bro, the whole three hundred and fifty thousand dollars. Always nice doing business with you fam." He told me, sticking his hand out to give me a play. I stuck the bag of money under my seat, "You wouldn't be so tired from running around if you didn't smoke so much weed and drink like a fish. Plus, you wearing them big ass heavy chains on yo' neck, no wonder you're out of breath." I told him.

"Yes, maybe your right, I like to spend my money on the finer things in life... Speaking of spending money, with that money that you just stuck under your seat I want you to go get a new windshield. How you riding around killing niggas and you got bullet holes all in yo' whip?! As a matter of fact, scrap this mothafucka and get yo'self a something new and fancier! You see that right there parked in my garage? That's that 2011 Audi BAL. You gotta' ride luxury like me dog!" Killa Kam told me.

I looked at him like he was crazy. Nigga, are you drunk?! This is 2010 vCharger, the R/T one! All I gotta' do is go get me a new windshield, then patch them bullet holes up, and I'm all good. Killa Kam's phone rang, "Yea, whatever Nigga, look; I gotta go and sell them bricks, so get wit' me a lil' later bro so we could have a few drinks. He told me, giving me play before stepping out of my ca.." I reminded him that I didn't drink, and he laughed, telling me that one day he would get me to have a drink with him.

"Oh yea, hey dog... My Graduation from UC3 is in just a couple of days, and you better be there. You know I'm expecting you!" I told him. With his phone to his ear, he grinned, "Fasho Nigga, you know I wouldn't miss that for nothing, Bro. That's funny, doe, a killer is graduating from college; that's fuckin'priceless!" He said, walking away and laughing.

Headed back to Detroit, I stopped at a red light when some pretty women pulled beside me. They looked like they wanted to talk to me until they saw the bullet holes in my car, and they shot up the windshield. I still rolled down my passenger window, "Whassup ladies, what yall about to get into?" I asked. The light turned green when the girl that was driving turned her face up at me and said, "Into somebody that's not dodging bullets!" and pulled off, leaving me looking stupid. I drove off questioning if my car was really all that bad, even though it was only a year old. I began adding numbers up inside my head and realized that I actually could afford to buy myself a brand-new car and still able to put away the majority of it. I could spend anything between sixty to eighty thousand dollars on a new car that was hot yet still didn't call for too much attention. I then headed to a dealership that was across the eight-mile road where Tiger was squeezing a car dealership owner, so I could get me a great price without being taxed.

I pulled off the dealership lot in a 2011 triple black Cadillac Escalade Truck that was fully loaded, tinted with five percent tint, which was the darkest that it came, and I bought some 28inch rims that were the same color as the car. The truck was originally priced at seventy thousand dollars, but I was able to get away paying him only forty thousand dollars being that I was connected to Tiger. Not wanting to give up on my Charger, I left it there and paid for it to be repainted a different color and had a new windshield put in it. Now I was riding good in my new truck I bought on my own.

It was my first step toward my independence and made me feel more like a man.

I felt so good riding in my truck that I was determined to be seen in it. I scrolled down my phone book and decided to dial Madison up finally. I was nervous as hell to call her, and for some reason, I was surprised that she had answered. I think a part of me was hoping that she didn't answer. I pulled myself together, told her who it was that was calling her, and after all of the "HOW YOU DOING'S" and good to hear from you's I asked her if she was busy so that we could hook up. She told me that she was actually free at the moment and was downtown at the Riverwalk, with a few of her sorority sisters taking a walk. I told her that I would be there shortly before we both hung up. I was geeked like a high school teenager; I got to brush my hair, fixing my clothes and making sure that I was presentable before I pulled up on her.

After finally finding a parking spot, I saw Madison standing nearby with three of her friends and waiting for me to get out of the truck. As usual Madison was beautiful as ever. She wore a sundress that was strapless, her hair was pinned up in a bun, and she wore sandals that showed her pretty feet off. I hopped out of the truck, unable to hold back my smile as I approached her. It was funny because I could tell that she was trying to hide her smile just as I was. I opened my arms for and a hug, and she smelled so good. Her arms wrapped around me felt so right, and I did not want to let her go.

"Wow, that is a nice truck, is it your's?" Madison asked me. I looked back at it and chuckled, answering yes it was. I then told her how beautiful she was, and after she thanked me and told me how handsome I was.

Her friends saw that she would be busy, so they told that they would catch up with her later on. I noticed that I didn't see her friend Ebony in the circle, that was who I was hoping to see. I still had unfinished business with her, so I planned to enjoy Madison's company for the time being. I still had to do my homework on Ebony who still had to be dealt with after witnessing me kill Trey. We both began walking up the Riverwalk kicking it and updating each other on how our lives been and what we were currently up to. She told me she was in Michigan State University and studying to be a paralegal. She also told me that she was working four days out of the week as an intern and that she was determined to have herself a career instead of settling for a job just so one could get by. "So enough about me, during the whole walk I've talked about myself and all you told me about yourself was that you been with Tiger and his asshole brothers for the last seven years. What do you do in your free time? What do you do for income? Tell me something about yourself, Romello." Madison asked me to do.

Hesitant to tell Madison that my life had consisted of a lot of murdering people I didn't know or care to harm, I tried answering her question the most subtle way possible. I told her only the good part, like that I was a part-time student that was soon to graduate from

Wayne County Community College and studying Journalism. I told her that after I graduated, I planned on enrolling at Michigan State University. I also told her that for employment, I did not have a specific job, but Tiger would pay me to do small favors for him from time to time. Madison stopped walking and gave me a look, "Well, going to school is very good Romello, I love seeing people from the hood trying to get out of it but doing favors from time to time for Tiger? Really? If his favors pays well enough for you to buy a new truck, then I am sure that I don't even want to know what it is that you're doing for him." She responded. Madison was far from stupid; she grew up around Tiger and knew that nothing he did was a legit hustle.

I shamefully shook my head at my current occupation, "Yes, I know, please believe that I'm working on a change. It's actually all in the works, but I need you to be patient with me." I replied back. She continued walking with me, "I hope so, Romello, especially if we plan on building some type of relationship together. I don't want to be with you and have to watch over my shoulders or anything like that. Madison said. T chuckled. One thing is for certain, and two things are for sure, I'm very respected on you would never have to worry about anything like that when you are with me." I assured her.

She smiled, "Well, that's good to know. She responded as we stopped at Coldstone Ice cream Parlor, where we continued to talk. We finished enjoying our ice cream date and as we headed back to her Chevy Impala, there

☐

wasn't a better time to ask her, but I needed to find whatever I could about her friend Ebony. "Soo, what was yo' girl name again that was trying to get you to drink with her at the titty bar the other night? I didn't see her with your other sorority sisters." I asked. Madison then exhaled before telling me how Ebony had experienced a traumatic situation where she was in the house with her boyfriend, who was killed, and so was one of her friends down the stairs in the kitchen. She told me that one of her boyfriend friends that was there also had been shot as well but survived. Hearing this story, I acted totally shocked at what I was being told but still interested in what had happened.

"So she survived something that crazy. Is she alright? Did she recognize the shooter and tell the police? Do the police have any suspects?" I asked, sounding concerned. Madison told me that she was fine but still shaken up not wanting any company or wanting to go anywhere. The police said that they would give her a few days to pull herself together since she was so emotional about what had happened they said they would call for her to visit the station a little later so she could make a statement. She told me that the only thing that Ebony knew was that the shooter wore a Detroit fitted cap and had braids. I stood there in a completely different zone, thinking about all that she was just telling ma.

"Hey. you okay?" Madison asked me. I snapped out of my daze and told her that I was good and how happy I was that we met up with each other. She smiled, "Awww, I'm happy that we met up too. I'll be in the city for another week you should hit me up again when your free." she told me. "Fasho, fasho.. Well, today is what, Thursday? How about we go out on Saturday on a real date this time?" I asked. She continued to smile, "Yes, I guess we could do that. Saturday would be just fine." She answered.

I stepped closer to her with arms open for a hug; she then opened her arms as well, giving me the most comforting hug I had in a long time. I shut her car door after she stepped in and told her to drive safely and to call me when she made it home.

I hopped in my truck, feeling anxious about the new relationship that Madison and I were building on. I couldn't wait until Saturday for our date. Maybe then I could find out more about Ebony, and if I was lucky enough, I would be able to find out where she lived. There was no way that I was letting her make a statement to the police.

Tiger Talk

10

When I pulled up in my driveway and seen Tiger's car parked in front of the house, all I could do was shake my head. I was so sick of the unwanted pop-up visits that I didn't know what to do. He probably was here to discuss the hit that I did on Trey; I haven't spoken to him since he gave me the assignment. I just knew that he wanted to grill me about how things went wrong, and more people ended up being killed than it was supposed to. Truth be told, I wasn't people ended up being killed feeling Tiger or his brothers anymore, and the only reason that I was still around them was because I felt indebted to them for taking me in after I killed Nate. If it wasn't for them, there is no telling where I would've ended up. I been nothing but loyal to Tiger and his brothers, but the fact that Tiger didn't want to pay me anything more than the five thousand dollars for the bodies that I was putting down made me look at him in a completely different light. He was a millionaire and didn't want to give me a raise for the murder missions that he assigned me to do. I didn't know exactly when, but I knew for sure that I would not continue to live under Tiger nor his Brother's.

I walked in the house, and there was Tiger looking through my folders where I kept my apartment/condo catalogs at. "Whasup Lil' Mello? You plan on moving or something sometime soon? Why you didn't tell me about this?" He asked. I closed the door behind myself, "Ummm, I was looking for a new place, but haven't found one just yet. Why, whasup?" I asked, walking toward him, taking my folders from his hands. "What, this house ain't good enough for you no more?" he asked, taking a seat at the kitchen table. I told him that I was just getting older and ready for my own place, plus I told him how I hated how his brothers would come over all the time like this was a party house. He nodded his head like he understood where I was coming from and told me that he would talk to them again about respecting my house.

"So... I heard things got hectic the other night on the

⁇

mission. two dead, one shot in the neck, and one got away. Now how did you let a girl get away from you?" Tiger asked. "Look, things got crazy, but I will handle it. Madison is friends with the girl, and somehow someway I will find out how I could get to her and shut her up." I answered. Tiger began shaking his head, "Yea, you better man, you cannot give that girl a chance to tell anyone what happened that night. You most definitely don't want her to make a statement and describe you, even if you were wearing a wig and all of that shit. Just get yo' girl Madison's phone, so you could get her phone number, and we could find out where it is she lives and all of that so you could handle her before it's too late."

Tiger told me, tossing me a stack of five thousand dollars. Tiger stood up and walked over to the window to take a look outside, "Hmmm,that's a nice truck Lil' Mello, 2011 too. How you get that?" He asked me.

I told him that I had just bought it with some of the money that I been saving from the jobs. He nodded his head and chuckled as he paced back and forth on the living room floor, "Hey ummm, you take anything from that nigga Trey's house that night? some work? some money? some jewelry?" Tiger asked. I learned from some of the best liars ever, I looked him dead in the face and told him that I didn't. "Hmm, well, Trey's lil' crew put the word out on the streets that whoever finds out who has their work or Trey's jewelry that they would pay a quarter million for whoever tells where they got it from.

Sooo..." Tiger was saying until I cut him off, "That ain't got shit to do with me, bro. I told him.

94

He nodded his head again, "Lil' Mello, you been up under my care for the past seven-eight years now, and if you learned anything about me, it's that I'm loyal to my family and would take care of the people that I love. I know that your loyal to my brothers and me and would do anything for us, right?" Tiger asked. Without hesitation I answered yes.

For some reason, I just knew that he was about to tell me that he knew that I took all the stuff that was missing from Trey's house. My heart was beating faster and faster, "I heard that fuck boy Shadow been trying to recruit you and..." He was saying before I stopped him again. "I would never leave you and join no other crew. Yea, he was trying to get me, but I ain't going nowhere!" I told him.

He smiled, "I already know. We family. We all we got!" Tiger said, sticking his hand out to give me a play. I gave him a play, and we gave each other man hugs sealing our loyalty towards the other. Tiger was getting ready to leave when I stopped him, "Yo' Tiger... I graduate from UC3 on Tuesday and wanted to invite yall to come through if yall ain't busy?" I asked him. He grinned, "Didn't I just tell you that we family? Of course, I would be there, are you crazy?" he said before walking out of the house. I smiled, and for the first time in a long time, I felt like we were actually a real family. I stood there in the front door watching Tiger get in the car when he rolled down the window, "Oh yes, don't move just yet aight? Imma' holla' at them fools one more time." Tiger said. I just nodded my head and shrugged my shoulders, "Ummm, aight man. I told him.

Grown man

11

Saturday Night

I sat parked outside of Madison's father's house, waiting on her to come out for our date, and I was fresh to death. Going out with Madison had been a dream of mines since I was a kid, and now that the opportunity had presented itself, I was going to do it right. I wore black from head to toe for tonight's event, black Polo fisherman hat, black and gold Cartier frames on my face, flat diamond earrings in my ear, a black polo t-shirt on with my Cuban-linked gold chain sitting on top of it. I had a gold Rolex on my wrist, black Polo linen shorts, and was wearing my black Prada's on my feet. The plan was what the average date had consisted of, which was a dinner and a movie. I also had to be cautious of the fact that at any given time, her phone could be left around me, and that would be my shot to get her friend Ebony's number from it.

Tonight was a night where business and pleasure was for sure to conflict with the other. walked down the street a couple of houses away so we could talk. "So have you thought about my offer, and what we talked about the other night?" Shadow asked me. I exhaled, "Look Shadow; I can't hold you up, I got mad respect for you and your brother because yall are the Hood's Big Homies but...Tiger and his brothers have become my family over the years, and my loyalty is with them. I'm going to have to decline your offer to join your team respectfully." I told him. I could tell that he was a bit disappointed, "Well, one thing I could respect is your loyalty with who has been loyal to you, and I can't be mad at your decision. Now what I do need you to know is that changing, and Tiger is bout' to start losing all of his business in the streets. There will be a war, and I was just calling myself inviting you to join the team that will win, that's all." Shadow told me. Madison stepped out of the house and looking amazing, "I hear you and appreciate the heads up, good luck back to you." I told him before opening my Passenger door for Madison.

After Madison and I left the movie theatre, we stopped at Benihana's Restaurant for dinner. I was proud to have an attractive woman such as Madison riding passenger who carried herself like a well-mannered and self-made boss.

She was so fine I couldn't keep my eyes off of her. She wore her hair straight down, her make-up was flawless, and she had a cranberry short V-Neck type of dress that showed mad cleavage, and her diamond necklaces sat right on top. She also wore some cranberry heels that complimented her well-built body frame; Madison had heads turning from both the men and women. It wasn't only hard for the public, but it was also hard for me not to stare at her ass that looked the fattest in the dress she had on. We sat there enjoying our meals and just talking about life and how we wanted so badly to be done with Detroit. She was tired of her brothers living in the street, bringing all their street heat home to her now sick father.

She just wanted to be able to make enough money to move all of them out of the city and live happily ever after, but she clearly wanted what everybody always dreamed of. I told her that I understood but some things as bad as we wanted to change, they just couldn't because they just want the time for it too. I encouraged her to continue loving and helping her family but to make sure that she took care of herself first. She smiled, appreciating the advice I had just given her, "So Mr. Romello, tell me why it is you do not have yourself a girlfriend?" She asked me. "Truth be told, I never had a girlfriend in my life. Wow! Now that I think about it, this is the first real date that I have ever been on." I told

?

her. Her jaw dropped to the table, "So you never had a girlfriend before, and this is your first date? So I'm your first date?" she asked. I nodded my head, answering yes. I thought about it I was even in shock, the only sex that I ever had was from the hoes that Tiger and his brothers would pass on to me."

"Aww that's cute, I feel so special. So are you a virgin too?" She asked hesitatingly. "I answered. Madison shook her head in disgust, "Mmm..only whores, huh? Tiger and his brothers always been male hoes. How though. I'm in shock but actually admiring that your sort of a virgin. So this also means that you never made love either, huh?" Madison asked again. I put my head down embarrassed when she reached over, placing her hand on top of mines, "Don't be embarrassed Romello, it's good to hear there are still men out there that are not trying to do it to everything that walking. Besides, I think that it's cute." she told me. Madison placed her phone on the table, "Well, I have to visit the ladies' room. I'll be right back shortly." she said, leaving her purse in her chair and phone where it was. Now was the time for me to act; I grabbed her phone and went straight through her phonebook, finding Ebony's number. I quickly memorized it and put her phone back exactly where she left it. Now that the business part of the date was over, I wanted to learn more about Madison.

I wanted to know things like her favorite color, favorite restaurants, the music that she liked, and why she was single. When she came back from the ladies' room, I asked her. Madison's favorite color was green, her favorite restaurant was Red Lobster, she was a Beyoncé fan like crazy, and when it came to answering why she was single, she paused. "Why am I single??

Well, the reason I am currently single is because my ex-boyfriend was in the streets and was murdered; I haven't had a man since then.. That's why I'm encouraging you to keep going hard in school, pull away from Tiger and his brothers, and to just get out of the streets Romello. I mean, that's if you want to be involved with me, that is."Madison said, looking into my face with a hopeful grin. I smiled, reaching my hand over the table and placing it on hers. "I most definitely want to be involved with you, just give me a minute baby. I'm leaving the streets and Tiger and his brothers, but I have to get a few things together first." I replied. She then chuckled, making me ask her what was so funny. "It's just my ex-boyfriend use to tell me the same thing, but okay. I guess I could give you a chance." She said to me.

We pulled back up to Madison's house, and the block was quiet and settled, Well... I had a good time with you tonight, Madison. I'm looking forward to our next date." I told her as I looked over to her. She smiled, "I really enjoyed myself to Romello; I feel so special that I'm your first date." She told me with a smile on her face. We both leaned over towards the other, giving each the biggest hug a before she stepped out of the truck. I told her that I was graduating from Community College on Tuesday and wanted to invite her. A big smile spread across her face, "Oh my god, you're just now telling me that you're graduating on Tuesday, and we been together all night?! Congratulations Romello! Wow, we would have celebrated more if I knew that! I am very impressed, of course, I would be there." Madison answered.

Hearing how excited that she was, was comforting and to hear that she was impressed made me feel even better. "Did you tell Tiger and his brother yet?" She asked. I answered yes and that they planned on being there as well, "That's good Romello, having family there would be a great feeling." She told me before telling me goodnight and closing the door behind her.

As I pulled off, I had a big smile across my face; my night had been one of my best nights in a long time. Madison had given me a lot to think about as far as my life decisions and current occupation. I enjoyed being with Madison tonight, but there were other things that needed to be done before I got myself excited.

I Can't Let It Go!!

12

Sunday Night 11P.M

Thanks to iPhone and highly advanced technology, I found out where Madison's friend Ebony was living by tracking her phone's information. Madison told me that the police would be taking Ebony's statement in a few days, and I couldn't chance her even to describe my disguise. Plus, I felt sloppy by leaving a witness alive, so it was a must that I paid her a visit to make sure that her statement could never be given room; I'll be right back shortly."

⁉

I crept in her backyard, knowing this could be a difficult mission by living with her parents and siblings. I hid behind Ebony's house looking for the bedroom that she lived in, and out of nowhere, a rottweiler silently attacked me, biting me on the leg. It was so painful that I automatically yelled but quickly caught myself remembering the mission I had at hand. While being attacked by the big dog, I pulled out one of my knives and began stabbing it numerously until it released its grip on me and fell to the ground beside me.

"Bo-Bo! Where are you at you stupid dog?!" Ebony yelled through the opened window. I pulled my pistol out, so if I was seen, I would just shoot her directly in the face. Her father must have stopped at Ebony's bedroom door because I heard a male's voice urging for her to get to bed early because the next day would be a busy one for her. He reminded her that she was meeting up with the homicide detectives then had to ride back up to her school to get the rest of her things. Ebony left her window and told her father that she had to shower before getting ready for bed. I heard Ebony close her bedroom door when I decided to peek in. She started undressing, revealing that sexy body that she had. Ebony was fine and had some very fine body features; it was just to bad that it was all about to go to waste. She had big titties and a fat ass, and all I could do was reminisce how good she looked when she had that threesome with Trey.

She put her robe on and grabbing the things needed for the shower before leaving her bedroom. With her window left cracked open, I lifted it a bit higher just enough for me to hop in. When I made it in without being detected? I tip-toed to her bedroom door, and right before I could close it, I heard Ebony's father from the other room asking where was the cold breeze coming from. Hearing his footsteps approaching the bedroom, I ran to her closet to hide. Ebony's father stepped into the bedroom, "This Girl..That's why it's cold in here." He said before closing the window and leaving the bedroom. I quietly exhaled in relief that I did not have to kill him. Now it was just a waiting game that I had play in order to know when the right opportunity was to kill Ebony.

Ebony walked into the bedroom after her shower and closed the door behind her. She then dropped her robe and began lotioning her naked body and putting sexy lingerie. It was ashamed such a female like herself had to trick off for the right price, but it was even more ashamed that I had to kill her. I pulled out the same knife that I killed her dog with and was getting ready to strike until her phone rang.

"Hello? Oh hi, Maddy girl, whasup? Nothing, just getting out of the shower about to get ready for bed. You know I got to go down to the police station in the morning to make my statement, I'm telling

you, I do not want to go. Right, I guess so... Well, girl let me gon' head and get some sleep, I'll call you tomorrow. Love you too. Bye." Ebony said before hanging up the phone.

Ebony then hopped in her bed and got under her blankets when her parents both came to her door, telling her how proud they were of her for making a statement on Trey's behalf. They began telling her that it was the right thing to do and how strong she was for doing so. They told Ebony that they loved her and turned off her bedroom light before closing the door and leaving. Ebony then made herself more comfortable when it was time for me to perform. I quietly slid the closet door open and crept over to her bed, my shadow reflecting off of the wall, which made her around. I jumped on top of her putting my hand over her mouth and putting all of my weight on top of before stabbing her multiple times until she stopped moving.

After silently stabbing Ebony to death, I tucked her bloody body back underneath the blankets as if she had been sleeping peacefully. I backtracked the bedroom, making sure that I left no type of evidence laying around. I opened her bedroom window back open, preparing to leave when I stopped to look back at Ebony, I didn't only hate what I had just done, but I hated the killer that I had become. Now an educated female was dead, and I was sure Madison's heart would be broken when she heard. Things had to change; I don't know how much longer I could do this.

I'm Here For You

13

Monday Afternoon

I pulled away from my school with my cap and gown in my backseat on which should have been one of my proudest days ever, but it wasn't. I was tired of what my life had consisted of and became, and for some reason, I felt like it would only become worse. Today I had decided that I would no longer murder people for Tiger or any amount of money. I refused to be a hitman any longer, and I didn't care what Tiger, or his brothers would say about my decision. I knew Tiger would surely be pissed about it, but if he really considered me family like he said he did, then he would understand where I was coming from.

I had no problem continuing to be the crew's muscle, and bodyguard whenever we went out, but that was the most that I was going to do. Hopefully, I would be accepted into a good college, and then I would no longer even have to do that for them. My cell phone vibrated in the cup holder when I saw Madison's name pop up.

I just exhaled loudly, getting ready to snap into my character before answering. She was hysterical, breathing hard, crying, and barely could even speak, telling me that she had lost her best friend Ebony. I gave her directions to my house and told her to come visit me in person. She agreed to come over and told me that she would be there in twenty minutes.

We both pulled into my driveway at the same time, and I already expected this to be an emotional visit. Madison stepped out of her car in a pair of gray jogging pants, Nike Flip-flop sandals, a white t-shirt, and her hair wrapped up in a bun. Even though her face was puffy from the crying that she had been doing, she was still the prettiest girl I ever seen. "Hey Baby, I'm sorry about your friend. Come here, gimme'a hug." I told her with my arms open. We stood outside my truck, hugging each other tightly, and the moment we separated from each other, I saw my ex-girlfriend Felicia sitting on Tabs porch smoking a cigarette with a mug on her face. I reached in my backseat, pulling out my cap and gown, "Awww Romello, I'm so sorry. This is supposed to be a good day for you, and I'm ruining it with my bed news and energy. I can't wait to see you

walk across that stage tomorrow." Madison told me as we walked up to my front door. I just nodded my head, telling her not to worry about it, and I couldn't wait to walk across the stage too. "Yo Romello, that's your truck?" Tab yelled over to me. "Yes, whatup?" I returned the question. "Oh shit... I was thinking about buying me one of those too." He added as if we were friends or something. I sarcastically laughed, "Nawl Homie, This truck's outta yo league. Keep driving your old school." I told him before Madison, and I stepped into my house. Madison chuckled, "Ohh, why you stunt on that man like that? She asked me. I told her I did it because he was a clown.

"Excuse the mess in here. Them niggas Shark and Pit think because they have keys that they could just come and go as they please." I told her as I led her to my bedroom. I just figured that I would share a great stress relieving tactic to one of my good friends, thats all." I answered with a grin on my face as well. Sha then stared into my face as if she was trying to read me, "Right, right...all I guess I would take the basic Massage Package for now just to see if your good with your hands. Then if your good I would decide if I want the premium package or not. Now where do you want me?" She asked standing to her feet and picking up the Grey Goose bottle taking a shot to the head.

I told her to lay across my bad but not before she taken har shirt off. When I told her to take her shirt off, she was ready to start talking shit but before she had a chance, I asked didn't Real Masseuse request the same thing before they would start. Knowing that I made a good point, she asked if I had any soothing smooth music that we could listen to. I handed her the remote that connected to my IPOD and sound system, then she pulled her shirt over her band and put her hands on her hip striking a pose on me.

I looked Madison up and down admiring her flawless body, I loved how her Titties set up in her bra ice and perky. "You better ba as good as you say you are!" She told me before laying down across my bed like I told her. I quietly exhaled in attempts to hold my composure. I would hate for me to have an erection poring her while gave her a massage Madison laid across my bed facing the big picture sized mirror allowing us to look at each other while the Massage was going on. She turned the music strict to the slow Jam section and turned on Usher's "TRADING PLACES song,

I climbed up on the bad mounting Madison like she was Bull, "Alright now, feel a lil poke back there than I know something." She said with a slight chuckle. "One things for sure and two things for certain, if you feel something, I guarantee that it would not be a "Lil'" poke." I promised her. She closed her eyes, "Yes okay, I guess we will find out shortly then huh?" she replied.

"I'm always on the top, tonight I'm on the bottom, cuz' we're trading places. When I can't take no more, tell me you ain't stopping, cuz' we trading places."

Usher sang through the speakers while I began massaging Madison. I firmly caressed her from the neck down to her lower back. Watching the faces, I saw her making through the mirror reflection and the moans that she made. I could tell that she was enjoying it. "Mmmm, damn that feels good, Romello. I guess you are pretty good with your hands, huh? I should have gotten the premium package if I knew that you were this good. She said with her eyes closed shut. To hear that she was considering the premium package made me begin to get anxious, "Would you unsnap my bra for me and get up under that area?" She asked. I told her no problem when in fact, it was, I unsnapped her bra and placed it beside me, massaging the sides of her breast. I knew what actually laid underneath her body. I tried my best to keep control of myself, but I couldn't hold the monster that was rising from inside of my shorts.

Following behind the Usher song was Avant's "Read Your Mind," and if only Madison could actually read my mind, she would be a bit shocked in what I was thinking. Then all of a sudden Madison asked me to lift up, I quickly got up and tucked away my erection facing upward toward my navel. Madison turned over in the bed, covering her chest with her unsnapped bra; her eyes were low from the liquor she had consumed. I could tell that she was tipsy and feeling real good at the moment. Not drunk nor sloppy and aware of all of her actions, "I think I'm ready for the Premium Package now, do you think you could handle it?" She asked me. I nodded my head, answering yes, "And I will handle it well." I answered her. "Good, do you think that you

?

could start with my feet please?" She requested before standing to her feet and removing her jogging pants. She laid back down flat on her back with her chest covered wearing only her boy-shorts and the polish on her pretty toenails.

"I can read your mind, babe; I know what you're thinking. It's alright. It's alright. It's alright, babe." Avant's voice echoed throughout the bedroom. I sat there in my bed with Madison's pretty feet in my lap while I massaged them, "Ohhh, yes, Romello, Oh my God, that feels amazing!" She moaned with her head, facing the ceiling and eyes closed.

"I told you I was going to handle everything, didn't I?" I replied. "Not Quite everything yet." She whispered in a low tone. Meanwhile, I couldn't help but admire Madison's perfect body, her petite frame, big thick thighs, smooth skin, and flat stomach all was making my mouth moist. I went from rubbing her feet up to her, calves all the way up to her thighs where I applied more pressure. I took my time massaging one thigh at a time and using both hands while doing it. After giving her thighs the proper attention, I couldn't neglect her inner thighs. That was the part that certainly aroused Madison because she began to shiver and squirm, unable to stay still. That's when she grew tired of covering her chest and threw her bra on the floor, exposing her beautiful and perky breast.

"Is it me or is it getting hot in here? Oh my God, I'm getting hot, Romello." Madison said, seductively putting one of her fingers in her mouth. She did not have not one bead of sweat on her body but was on fire with hormones raging and yearning for my touches. This physical interacting was not only affecting her but affecting me as well. I was hot as soon as she took her pants off and got into my bed, and now that I was staring at her perky and nice sized breast, I was on fire, and erection could no longer be hidden. Realizing that she had just exposed her breast to me, she covered them up as much as she could with her forearm and covered her eyes with her other hand.

"I can't believe I'm showing you my body and letting you massage me, oh my God!" She said feeling embarrassed. Not wanting her to regret what was going on, I reached for her forearm that she was using to cover her chest. I smoothly removed it away from what she was covering, "Listen, no need to feel embarrassed, Madison. It's just me, the same nigga that's been in love with you since we were kids. I'm the same nigga that's still in love with you right now. Just relax...Get comfortable and accept what's taking place at this moment. For this is a magical moment that I am sure neither one of us would regret. That's a promise." I told her in my strong and smooth tone.

She exhaled, removing her hand from her face; I could tell at that moment that she was letting her guards down and decided to trust me. I mounted Madison's body again and slowly leaned down, placing my lips onto hers's kissing her passionately. Her lips felt and tasted so good that I never wanted to stop but I had to continue to pleasure the rest of her body. I kissed from her lips to

?

her neck then down to her big, pretty perky breast when I took my time giving each one of them the tender care that they deserved.

I sucked her breast softly when she placed both hands on the side of my head and whispered for me to bite her nipples. Now sucking on her succulent breast and biting on her nipples, I continued going down her body all the way down to her waist. I slid her boy shorts down only to see a perfectly shaven vagina. I never in my life had given a woman oral sex before, but I knew after seeing Tiger's brothers do it to the women that had bushes that I know whenever I did do it that I wanted it to be bald like the one in front of me. This was the best-looking vagina that I ever seen.

This was Madison, my first crush so I was going all out, I stood up, removing my shirt, showing her how nice and well in shape I was. Her eyes grew big, seeing all of the muscles and tattoos, but when I took off my basketball shorts and my brick hard dick standing every bit of nine and a half inches, her eyes really opened. "Damn Romello, who would've known you were in such good shape and packing that Mandingo warrior inside them shorts! Mmmm-mmm." She said, still never taking her eyes off of me with a grin on her face.

I stood there, smiling proud of what I been blessed with, "You think you could handle this?" I asked, referring to my Penis. "I don't know, but I'll try, and you better not hurt me."

She answered, lifting her fist up, indicating she would

hurt me. I continued kissing her from her waist down to her pussy and went straight to work. I started kissing then licking on her clitoris with both hands up and under her cuffing and squeezing on her ass cheeks. Madison could not help but moan and scream my name while trying to squirm up the bed. "Romello, Romello, Romello Oh my God babe, right there! Ohhh yea...right there! Ohh...shit! Yes! Yes! Yes! Mmm-hmmm, Yes, Baby!" She moaned and scream. Hearing her moan and scream, enjoying the oral sex that I was performing on her, was only hyping me to go harder. I began sucking on her clitoris, then I would spit on it right before sucking on it again. All of a sudden, both of her thick thighs squeeze my head, locking me in between when she began shivering and quivering rapidly. She had cum all inside of my mouth and on my face. After her thighs finally released me, I stood up short of breath. I looked down at her face, and she was certainly pleased. "How was that for a first-timer?" I asked with a smile on my face flopping on the bed beside her. "Oh my! God, that was your first time?! Your lying!" She accused me as she sat up. I nodded my head, answering that indeed it was.

"Wow! I'm impressed, tell me what you think about this afterward then." She told me as she leaned down, taking my dick and stuffing as much as she could inside of her mouth. Madison sucked on my dick like it was a bomb pop icicle, and she was very good at it. She Licked on it up and down, sucked, and kissed the head, even coming all the way down where she began to lick and suck on my balls. Sending of a sensitive pleasure that I very much enjoyed. Then Madison got a little fancy with it and began jerking my shaft with both hands while sucking on the tip. After a while I was unable to take anymore, I had to damn near snatch the dick from her warm mouth to prevent me from cumming so fast. I couldn't cum so fast during our first time ever having sex, so I had to pull away.

Waiting to see her face while having sex, I directed Madison to lay flat on her back for the missionary position. Right before I was about to insert my brick hard python inside of her, she raised her fist up at me again, "Remember, if you hurt me with that big ole' thing, I will punch you!" Madison threatened. I assured her that the last thing that I would ever do is something that would hurt her.

Xscape, "The softest place on Earth" echoed through the bedroom when I slowly placed my dick inside her tight pussy. Her pussy was so tight that it would only allow not even half of my dick inside of her. I leaned down and began kissing her again, but this time, I was tongue kissing her, which was a lot more intimate and bought a hot new different vibe to the sex that we were having.

"Mmm-mmmm, Ohhh Romello, Mmmm, I love you." Madison whispered into my ear while I was inside of her. Without hesitation, I told her that I had loved her too. Once we told each other that we loved the other, it had changed the tone of our sex, and it had become lovemaking. Her pussy was now allowing more and more of me inside of her, which allowed me to speed up and making her hold on to the sheets with a tighter grip. "Ohhh-Ohhh, promise me you won't hurt me." She moaned loudly. "I promise!" I told her while pounding on her soaking wet pussy. "Do you really love me? Do you really love this pussy?!" She asked in screams. "I love you; I really love you! I love dis' pussy! Do you love dis dick?" I answered her and returned with my demands. "Ohhh shit! I love dis, dick! I love the dick!" Madison yelled back.

"I'm bout' to cum! m cumming!" I yelled, continuing to fuck her brains out. Madison on then tightly wrapped her legs around me, locking me inside of her pussy, forcing me to release all of what felt like an ounce of semen. I flopped right beside Madison as we both laid naked short of breath in my bed. We were both silent, and I was sure we were both shocked by what had happened between us. Madison then slid closer toward me and laid her head on my chest, "So... Did you really mean all the things you were just saying while...you know, we were doing it?" She asked.

Staring up to the ceiling, "of course, I meant everything I said when I told you that I loved your pussy." I answered jokingly. Madison punched me in the chest, making me laugh even more and telling me to stop playing so much. "Nawl but forreal, all jokes aside..I meant everything I said. The question is, did you mean everything you were saying to me while we were making love?" I returned the question and correcting her statement. She began smiling, "Yes, I meant it, I wouldn't have said if I didn't mean it." She answered.

It felt good knowing Madison, and I felt the same way about each other, that must have been the feeling that we realized we both had when we first tongued. I realized how much I cared for her and what she meant to me. "So what's next? Do we date, or are we together? What?" she asked.

"Well, I guess I have to tell all of my ladies that they can no longer just be popping up unannounced no more because I have myself a girl now," I answered again jokingly. Madison hit me with a rib shot, "So we are together than, huh? Sound good to me."Madison said, looking up to me with a smile on her face. Sounds great to me, I been waiting for forever to call you mines." I replied.

Overwhelmed with the news that we were in a relationship, she leaned up closer toward my face and planted her soft lips upon mines. I then pulled the blankets over both of our bodies, and we curled up in the spooning position together, holding tightly to one another.

This felt like a dream to me; not only did I just make love to the girl I been in love with since I was a kid, but now we were in a relationship, and I could call her mines. This was my first real relationship ever.

Stay Focused

14

I woke up to the sounds of whimpers and cries, and when I reached for where Madison was laying, she was no longer there. I sat up, opening my eyes, realizing that the cries were coming from the bathroom. I got up and walked over to the closed bathroom door when I knocked, asking Madison if she was okay. "Huh? Ohhh, yes, yes I'm fine, I'm okay. I will be out in a minute." She answered, trying to mask her crying voice tone. I slowly opened up the door, and there she was sitting on the bathtub railing with tissue in her eyes from crying. I sat across from her on the toilet and reaching over, putting my arm over her for comfort. "I can't believe that my friend is gone." She cried. I hugged her tightly, telling her that everything would be okay, but on the inside, I felt terrible that she was going through this because of me. "I need you to find out who did this to her Romello, please." she cried to me laying her head on my shoulder.

My doorbell then rang, interrupting our moment, "You're expecting someone?" Madison asked. I told her that I wasn't and that I would be right back. I walked to the front door, and it was Tiger on the other side. This was a first Tiger never rang the doorbell before and normally would just walk in with his key. Turning to face Madison I headed to the see about the door. Opening the door, I came face to face with Tiger and his crew who signalled for me to meet them outside. Stepping out I closed the door behind me and was handed a single piece of paper." I need you to handle this for me, this is the mark, his contact information.

Knowing I really didn't want to I fixed my face to speak but was interrupted by Tiger. "Listen I need this handled and only you can take care of it. Listen I know you finna say no but check this out this is a job, and this will put money in your pockets. I exhaled and nodded my head, "Yea I know son, I know." Thinking it over I needed the needed that hundred thousand because that would put me one step closer to leaving Tiger and his brother's crew, and then I could go on with my dreams. I exhaled and nodded my head. "Yes, I'll do it. I got you. I answered. A big smile spread across Tiger's face, "Fasho then, get that money! Call me as soon as the deal is done, and I would bump into you afterward.

Tiger told me as he walked toward me, giving me a play before leaving the house. I closed the door behind him and kept questioning myself what was the catch to doing this deal for him. Why was Tiger so willing to pay me a hundred thousand dollars to do a job that I been with him to do on numerous occasions??

(6pm)

I turned down the block that the Mexicans lived on and pulled up in front of the house that Tiger would always pull up in front whenever they would do their transactions. Southwest Detroit was the home of the legendary BMF Crew and was known for gang-banging Mexicans that did not hesitate to kill. I was surely in the slums, but the worst part about it was that I was in their slums that they knew so well. Every time Tiger and I would come out here; there would be at least fifty Mexicans standing guard while they handled their business. I knew that I was a real killer, but with the numbers that they had, I couldn't help but be paranoid of my surroundings. The main Mexican Hector was a bald head, tattooed-up scary-looking guy that always would hop in the car with one of his little Mexican buddies but with me being who I was, I knew that he was his shooter, but we never minded.

I had my .40 Ruger with an extra thirty round clip attached to it sticking up under my left leg out of sight just in case shit had to get real. I rather been prepared than to be assed-out. Hector and his little Mexican buddy hopped in the car, and as usual, Hector was in the passenger seat, and the Little Mexican hopped in the back. I checked out the scenery, and unlike any other time there were at least a hundred Mexicans standing guard for this transaction. I didn't like how things looked one bit; I hated being outnumbered like this. I kept the car running and foot on the break, I was for from stupid and knew that at any time the car could be rushed and straight killed or robbed. Them Southwest Mexicans were just as Grimy as the niggas were.

Soon as Hector and the little Buddy seen that they were hopping in with only me in the car, they looked pissed. Hector asked why was I there instead of Tiger to do the deal, and I told him that I did not know but was only doing what I was told to do. "That fuckin! Vato is a piece of shit! He knows he sold me that bullshit the last time and he was pose' to make shit right for me this time! He couldn't even show his face like a man, that's why he sent you!"

Hector said in a pissed off tone. I told him that I agreed that Tiger was a piece of shit and that I was sorry that he got some bullshit the last time. I asked him if he still wanted to do the transaction that I was sent for because, if not, I could leave. Hector then told me to show him the work that he was supposed to purchase and promised me that Tiger was going to get what he had coming to him. "Fasho-Fasho, right... Ummm, you got the money, right? With all due respect, let's do this at the same time." I told him.

I didn't know if it was because he thought I was just a young ass worker that would be stupid enough to be got, but he showed a lot of attitude while pulling out the money that he was supposed to pay me with. I kept an eye on Hector, making sure that him or his little buddy in the back seat didn't try anything slick, but I also stayed in my mirrors watching out for his Mexican buddies, that were standing guard. When I saw the Stacks of money when I slowly reached under the seat pulling out the bag of work to exchange.

"I should be getting this shit for free after that last bullshit batch that he sold me. What all think, I'm some type of Puta' or something homes!?! Hector said, getting more hyped as he spoke. "I don't think your none of that big dog, Imma holla at Tiger, and tell that nigga to get you right," I told him, trying to calm him down, but it wasn't working.

Hector pulled out a pocket knife to test the product with the ugliest mug on his face, almost like he dared me to say something smart to him. He told me that he wasn't getting out of the car until he tasted the product, and I didn't mind because that gave me time to scan through the money to make sure that it was all there. He took a big snort of one of the bricks from his knife. "Ohhh..yes! Yes! Now that is what I'm talkin' bout, Now just let me test the other ones, and we are all set." Hector said, and finally relaxing. I counted the money, and it was all there, so I tucked it under the seat while he continued testing the work. He took an even bigger snort of the rest of the Bricks when he all of a sudden yelled and just snapped on me, tripping, "What the fuck is this?! This is not fucking heroin punta'! This is fuckin' sugar! NO! NO! NO! He continued yelling. I was totally confused and scared enough that I flicked the safety off of my Ruger that was still hidden underneath my leg. "Oh, you fucked up Vato! You're dead! A Carnales Maten an Este Hi Jo De La Chingada!" Hector opened his door, yelling out to his crew. I had no idea what he told his crew, but I did hear him tell me that I was dead before he got to speaking his Spanish.

Hector Crew that had to been at least a hundred deep, all got to clutching their weapons and approaching the car. The little buddy that was in the back seat began fidgeting, and I instantly panicked. I quickly drew my pistol fast as the men in the Western movies and directed it toward the back seat at the little Buddy firing my pistol four times. Hector seen what was going on and attacked me in the front seat, wrestling me for my pistol when I stomped on the gas. The passenger's side door opened, placing a separation between his crew and us that were on their way. We were speeding up a residential street still fighting for the possession of my gun when we smacked a parked car two blocks away from where we met. Hector's face smashed against the dashboard, and the airbag smacked me in the face making me dizzy by its forceful contact. Trying to shake off the pain I suffered. I looked at Hector, and his whole face was bloody as hell.

He looked like he had a broken nose, and I felt as if I had a concussion. I looked in the back seat and seen that Hector's buddy was leaning to the side with his eyes still open. I looked on the floor of the passenger's side, and there was my pistol that fell out of my hand on the impact. I looked in the rearview mirror at my busted lip I seen Hector's crew running up to assist their Mexican Brothers.

The first thing that I did was lean over to the passenger's side floor and picked up my gun when Hector started laughing like he was an evil villain, "You batta' kill me vato! You betta' kill me?" he said, spitting out a mouth full of blood. In any other situation, killing him would be easy, but I had a feeling that keeping him alive was the best route, I leaned over to open his door and pushed him out of the car, "I told you that I was doing what I was told, I ain't got no beef wit' you!" I told him. I reached in the backseat and pushed out his dead buddy beside him. Hector looked at me with a surprised look that I didn't kill him, and he had every reason too. With the car still operable, I backed up and made a getaway before his crew made it to me.

Soon as I pulled off, there were shots being fired at me, causing me to duck and try to dodge them. In my rearview mirror, I could see Hector standing to his feet and telling his crew to stop shooting.

I walked out of a Gas Station that was far away from Southwest with a limp, Evian water in my hand and flopped in the driver's side seat of the 300C that was all smashed and shot up. I couldn't believe all that just happened and that I made it out alive. After all that just went on, I just wanted to be someplace that I know was safe and I could take my mind off of the crazy stuff that I just experienced. I pulled my cell phone out of my pocket and dialed Madison up. She could tell by my tone that something was up, so she asked me if I was okay. "Ummm yeah, I'm fine. Just...Can I come and visit you?" I asked her.

"Sure, you do know that I'm up in Lansing at School, right?" She answered and returned a question. I told her that I know where she was, and without hesitation, she told me that she would love for my company up there. I told her that I would be up there in the next couple of hours and would call when I was close.

I put my phone in the cupholder when I looked on the floor of the passenger side and seen that the bag full of work that Hector claimed was fake was still in the car. I picked the bag of work up and tested what Bricks were real and fake. I wasn't even surprised that some of them were fake because I knew first hand that Tiger was a shady and grimy ass nigga. The fact that he sent me on his suicidal mission was foul and could not be forgiven. It all started to add up why he wanted me to go on this mission instead of his brothers. He knew that he sold Hector some bullshit before and that he would still be mad, and he knew he was going to try and sell some bullshit to him again but through me.

He didn't mind letting me keep a hundred thousand dollars. My mind was racing a thousand miles by the minute with many questions that needed answers. How could Tiger send me on that mission if he looked at me as family? Could he have known that she would get as real as it got? Could this have been a set-up toward me? Am I supposed to trust him after how he after how he just played me and almost having no killed? I headed home to get myself together before taking that two-hour trip to Lansing, Michigan. I even packed myself enough clothes to last a while, as well as my Safe that held my money. I had a lot to think about, but tonight I just wanted to be with someone that I know I could trust. As far as I was concerned, I was done with Tiger, and at the very moment, I quit...

Real Friend

15

11:15pm NIGHT BEFORE GRADUATION

During the drive to Madison's apartment, I was thinking of all the stuff that I needed to do since I no longer planned on working for Tiger or even going back to the house that he had me living in. I felt totally betrayed by the fact that I was sent on that mission, knowing that there was bad blood between him one of the Mexicans. There was no way he could have cared for me like a family would and had done me like that. I had enough, and my first step from separating myself from Tiger would be to get myself my own apartment far away from Detroit. Tiger agreed to come to my graduation and that was where I was going to tell him that I was done working for him. I was sure that he would be pissed about it, but he no longer had any say so. I'm a grown man now.

Madison answered her door wearing some super short pajama shorts, a wife beater that had her big titties and hard nipples clearly visible, and her hair was pinned up in headscarf with no earrings in her ear. As usual, Madison was still beautiful in my eyes, even when she wasn't trying. I stepped inside her place after giving her a hug and a kiss when I walked straight over to her to take a seat. When I looked around her place, I seen bags packed up, and Madison walked over, sitting beside me looking in the face noticing my busted lip asking me what had happened. I put on a smile and told her that I was okay, and just wanted to come and check on her to make sure that she was good. She gave me a funny look, "Okay, I believe that you may have wanted to come and check on me, and I appreciate it, but I could tell by your tone on the phone that something wasn't right. I could tell that something was not right because you just drove two hours to come and visit me when you graduate tomorrow. I also know that something is not right because you just limped in here trying to disguise it, and your lip is busted. Again I'm asking you Romello, what happened to you, and are you okay?" Madison asked me.

I sat there trying to put together an answer without telling her that I been a professional hitman that almost was just killed. "Look, I'm a real friend. You could talk to me, babe." Madison added. I exhaled, "I just decided that it's time for me to pull away from Tiger and his brothers. I... just can't keep dealing with them and their lifestyle that they lived and allowed me to live. It's just not conducive to my health or future, feel me? I'm straight on all of that shit, I packed up enough clothes to last me for a nice minute, and I'm going to find myself a new place." I told her. "There it is then... It's time for you to separate yourself from them. Especially with your life and health being in jeopardy. It's okay; he helped you when you were younger, so I see why there is an attachment, but your grown and educated young man now baby that has a bright future ahead of him. You were the one who made it through all the life challenging obstacles and adversities and that's why your walking across that stage tomorrow. With that being said, I will help you find yourself a place, and I'll help you detach yourself from Tiger and his brothers. You got me now babe. "Madison assured me.

I looked over at her and just smiled, all the things she said made so much sense. "What? What are you smiling for?" She asked me with a grin on her face. "Nothing, I'm just happy to have such a real smart friend beside me. I never met any female like you before." I told her. She started blushing and batting her eyelashes, "Well, you know...I do what I can do when I could do it."

Madison replied, making both of us laugh at her silliness. "Nawl but all jokes aside, If I could help you with anything, then I got you, and I know if I need you that you would have me as well," Madison said. I nodded my head in agreement "Well, I'm glad to know you got me and glad to you know that I have you too." I told her as I leaned over, kissing her soft lips.

"Mmm-mmm, you're a good kisser babe... How about this, you run down to your, you run down to your truck and grab whatever it was that you packed and then I would meet you in the bedroom. Deal?" Madison asked, now leaning over to me to kiss me.

"Hmmm, I guess so since your begging me and all," I responded with a grin. She laughed and stood to her feet, "Whatever, Boy, see you in a minute. "She said, removing her wife-beater right before heading to her bedroom. Anxious to get to her bedroom, I ran down to get my things out of the truck. Being with Madison wasn't only therapeutic, but it was a sure stress reliever. I was beginning to think that she was the best thing to ever come into my life.

GRADUATION

16

Next Day

Today was finally my graduation day, and besides all of the crazy things that had been happening in my life. One thing that I was proud of was how I was able to graduate Community College. I knew that if my parents were around that they would be proud of me and my accomplishments. As I sat in the stands with my graduating class, it was not hard to recognize my baby Madison and my friend Killa Kam who was sitting in the audience to support me. I looked all over the place, but there was not any sign of Tiger or his brothers in the building. I couldn't believe they were not here; it actually disappointed me that they weren't. It just further let me know that I was not considered a family to them.

After the Graduation Ceremony, Madison and Killer Kam took me out to celebrate at a new restaurant that was out in the suburban area. During the drive, I received a text message from

Tiger asking me where I was; I gave him the directions to where we would be. He texted back, telling me that they were on their way. Truth be told, I didn't think he was coming to celebrate with me, but he wanted to meet up with a to pick-up the money from that deal that I did with Hector yesterday. Then again, I would feel a little better seeing that Tiger and his Brothers were coming to celebrate with me after missing my graduation ceremony. I couldn't help but consider them as my family even though they were not treating me the same way. Madison, Killa Kam, and I all sat at our table laughing, talking, and enjoying our meals when Killa Kam told the waitress to bring over three bottles of Rose'. Three bottles of Rose in a restaurant were costly and when I told him that he didn't have to, he insisted that he did. "Look fam, you my dog, homie and my real friend... It's not every day that I know someone that graduates from college, so I'm proud of you, and I do have to do this; I still have a surprise for you that I'm waiting to give you after we finish our meals." Killa Kam told me. Appreciative of our friendship, I stood up, reaching over the table, giving him a play. Madison sat back, smiling, and admiring the bond that Killa Kam and I shared. She then asked, how did we become friends. I couldn't wait to tell her the story, and when the bottles came, I had myself a small drink before he got to tell the story. Madison under

?

my arm, leaning her head on my shoulder, listening to everything that he was saying. In the middle of the story being told, Tiger and his brothers, Pit and Shark, walked in the restaurant's door.

"We were the only two young niggas pulling into the school parking lot in our own cars, and at least two days out of the week, we would drive foreigns to school. We were the niggas all the girls wanted, but my nigga Mello here wasn't paying them any attention. We have been friends since back then. "Killa Kam finished. "Yea, I remember the days I use to let Lil' Mello ride my Bentley's, Porches, Benz's, and Range Rover's. He didn't even want to, but I wanted him to shine. Now that we know who's cars were driving?" Tiger jumped in the conversation while they all found them a place to sit at our table.

Killa Kam looked at them and then back to me with a look on his face like "Oh, this is the niggas you been telling me about.". I exhaled, "Ummm Killa Kam, these are the Big Bro's I told you about. That's Tiger, Pit, and Shark. Yall, this is a friend of mines, Killa Kam...Yall already know Madison."

I introduced everybody to each other. They all spoke to Madison, and I could tell that Killa Kam had jumped right into his defense mode being that I told him everything about Tiger and his brothers.

He knew everything from the moment that they took me into all of the murders that I was responsible for because that's what I was paid to do. I also told him how shady and grimy they all were, so he already felt a certain type of way toward them.

"Oh, okay, okay... These are your brothers who didn't even come and see you graduate, huh? Ohhh, and to answer your question. I was driving my uncle's foreign cars back then, but now I'm grown and getting my own money, so I drive my own, feel me? I know yall seen that new Maserati parked outside." Killa Kam said, being the stunner that he always been. One thing about my nigga Killa Kam was that he never cared about any kind of consequences, repercussions, or beef with anybody. He was a flashy, loud, cocky, and arrogant nigga that didn't take any shit from anybody and was ready for whatever.

Tiger sat back cool, calm, and collected, but Pit and Shark didn't take the sarcasm and arrogance from Kila Kam to well. "Oh, okay, we were wondering who's car that was out there. So you're getting money then, huh? How much? Pit asked. I already know what was coming on through their minds, but I wasn't playing it at all. "Hey, hey, hey Man... Everybody needs to chill out, pour themselves some of this Rose' we got here and just relax. We here to celebrate my graduation today, feel me?" I said intervening. "Yea yall, let's celebrate Mello graduating. For starters, I want to apologize for our absence.

Something very important prevented us from attending, but I promise that I'll make it up to you. So let's enjoy the evening, and Killa Kam, is it? It's good to meet you." Tiger said, sounding like the grown man that he was supposed to be. Killa Kam agreed with Tiger that we all should enjoy our evening, and to make up for his sarcasm, he ordered three more bottles of Rose' for Tiger and his brothers. After everybody ate, and glasses were filled with champagne, things seemed cool, and everybody was getting along. I even saw Tiger and Killa Kam share a few laughs and giving each other plays. For a brief moment, I felt what it was like to have a family. All the murders under my belt, the Ebony situation, branching off from Tiger, and almost being killed last night was the furthest thing from my mind. I just wanted this to be my life without all of the stress.

Killa Kam tapped his glass with a fork for everybody's attention, "Aight I told you that I had a surprise for you, and here it is, congrats fam!" He told me, handing me a gift bag from up under the table. As I opened the bag and pulled out the small box, I noticed everybody was watching to see what it was that I got. When I opened, it was Presidential Rolex Watch, "Awww shit, God Damn Bro!! A Presidential?! Really?! This had to run you at least thirty to forty thousand dollars. I said before taking it out of the box and putting it on my wrist. "Yes, it was only forty-two thousand, but it ain't nothing. Yo' mans is proud of you. In fact, I'm so proud of you that I talked to a couple of important people I know that just so happens to work at the Michigan State University Journalist/News Paper Department and he told me that as soon your accepted that he has a job to start you at. I know you always wanted to be a Writer/Journalist, so, yes, I did that for you. Congrats again, my nigga!"Killa Kam told me with a grin on his face.

Hearing that news had both Madison and I super excited and in shock. I damn near jumped over the table thanking Killa Kam giving him a man-hug for all that he's done for me. Him talking to a Michigan State Program Director that could help me get my foot in the door to become a Writer/Journalist was a huge deal and more important than any gift that I could ever receive. After hugging Killa Kam and kissing Madison, I seen Pit and Shark still admiring my watch and Tiger sitting there with a phony smile on his faces as if he was happy for me. Tiger's phone rang loudly throughout the

[?]

restaurant when he looked at it and silenced it, "Alright everybody, I had fun spending time with yall, but we have some business to attend to. Killa Kam, nice to meet you and lil it's always good to see you as well. Um Lil' Mello, could I holla. at you for a few seconds?" He asked me.

Tiger and I stepped to the side where no one could hear what it was we were discussing, "How did last night go with that fuckin' Mexican out in Southwest? He didn't give you any problems, did he?" Tiger asked me. Hector must of never called between me and them.

Work that Tiger tried to sell him. That's not how Mexicans handled their business anyway; when they were ready to ride on someone, they would do it, without warning. "Ummm, it went straight. Why wouldn't it?" I returned the question. " No reason, I was just asking. So you got the money?" He asked in excitement. When I answered yes, he damn near jumped out of his skin.

"Okay, bet, where is the money?" Tiger asked. I told him that it was in my truck and under the seat. Aight, I'll grab it..Yo'. So I stopped by the house last night, and since I didn't see your truck I pulled all the way up into the backyard and noticed the 3000. You had an accident last night?" He asked.

I told him that I dodged a dog in the street and smacked right into a parked car committing a hit and run. "I looked inside the car and seen cocaine in the front seat, what was that about?" Tiger asked. Coming back with the perfect answer, I told him that Hector stuffed damn near a whole brick of the work into his nose and must have gotten some on the floor. Tiger just nodded his head but knowing that he did not care whatever had happened. He was so happy that he had his money that he really could care less. He then gave me a play and asked me if I was good, with a straight face, I answered yes. Little did he know that I had already planned to stop working for him, but I just did not want to tell him at the time.

Tiger and I stepped back over to the table where everybody else was at when he said his good-byes again and pulled out a loaf of money offering to pay for the tables bill. "Oh nawl, yall good. I got this one." Kills Kam told him.

Tiger gave Killa Kam a surprised look. "Okay then Killa, Yo' LIL Mello, I like yo' Mans here. He's cool peoples. C'mon yall" Tiger told his brothers. Both brothers got up and were making their way to the door when Pit stopped and took a look at Killa Kam. "Yo' kills, that's a nice Michigan Chain you got there. You mind telling me where you get it from?" He asked him. I looked at the chain and realized that it was one of the chains that I sold him that was in Trey's jewelry collection. This was my first time noticing it and couldn't believe that I never recognized it, so I could have told him to tuck it.

Oh, this Murder Mitten? I had one of my jewelers make this for me awhile back, but when I saw that he made a few people the same one, I stopped wearing it as much." Killa Kam answered. Pit nodded his head with a grin on his face when he looked over at me then back at Killa Kam. Pit had recognized the chain, and I could tell that he already had put it together that I sold it to him. Tiger and Shark stood at the restaurant's exit calling for Pit to come on, Killa Kam and I just looked at each other after they all left when he told me that he had totally forgotten that he had it on.

"What did you forget, Killa?" Madison asked him. He told her nothing; I Just hoped that Pit didn't create any new drama by telling Tiger what it was that he just saw. That would mean that Tiger and his crew would know that I been tucking things for myself whenever I killed somebody.

Alliances Built

17

I couldn't believe what I was doing, I never thought that I would be in Southwest ever again, but when I turned down Hector's block, it became real once again for I did not hundred Mexicans posted on the block, and all eyes were on my truck when I pulled up. Being that they could not see through my tinted windows and was in their neighborhood, they were ready to kill on sight. Of course, I had my pistol with the extended thirty round clip attached to it under my leg but that wouldn't even clear at least half of the Mexicans out if it went down between them and me. My purpose in even being here was to let Hector know that I was only the transporter during my last visit and meant no disrespect by what had happened. I also wanted to somehow make-up for killing his little Mexican Buddy, I just hoped that I made it out of this alive.

I rolled down my window and asked if Hector was around, and as soon as the question came from my mouth, there were at least fifty guns aimed directly

?

at my face. I lifted my hands up in the air, surrendering, "I have something important to tell him, and I also have something for him." I told them. An older Mexican recognized me from my last visit and stepped forward, "Oh, I remember you... You're the Vato from the other night! Yes, you killed my Nephew!

You fucked up Homes'!" He told me while pressing his pistol on my forehead with aggression. At this moment I had closed my eyes and second-guessed my decision on coming back to Southwest. "Hey, hey, hey Senor'... Let me see what this fool has to offer first. It has to be something spectacular for him to risk his life and come back here."

Hector said, making his way through the crowd. The old Mexican lowered his pistol from my forehead, and Hector stepped up to my Driver's side door. "You got big balls coming through, here again, Vato! What is it that you could possibly have for me? What is it that you could possibly want to talk to me about?" he asked. It was no secret that I was a bit shook; I never had so many guns drawn at me at one time in my life. These Mexicans could kill me and make me disappear without a trace.

I reached over to the passenger's seat, grabbing a bag, "I got the brick that you liked and a hundred thousand dollars for the trouble that I caused you."

I told him as I handed over the bag through the window. Hector sarcastically chuckled. "Oh you think that you could make things right for the other night or something Homes!? Tiger got me fucked up! Hector said, raising his voice and his crew cheering him on behind him. "No, No this is all me. Tiger doesn't even know that I'm here. I'm doing this all on my own, and I wanted to apologize." I said loud enough for everybody to hear me. When I apologized, Hector's entire crew grow silent and lowered their guns. Hector looked at me in the face and told me to step out of the truck.

Nervous about what was about to transpire. I was about to try and sneak tuck my pistol on my waist, "No need in trying to hide your gun, Homes', but if it makes you comfortable, you could bring it with you." Hector told me as he stepped away from the truck. When I stepped out of the truck Hector handed his crew the bag that I gave him and spoke their language before we began walking up to his block. As we walked, I noticed how organized his entire crew was; they were patrolling the entire block like they were military. "You could relax Vato; I'm not going to kill you. What's your name and how old are you by the way?" He asked me. I told him my name and age, and he chuckled in disbelief as to my age.

I must say... It's been heavy on my mind as to why

you let me live that day you could have easily killed me. Why was that?" Hector asked me. "I didn't kill you because I knew Tiger was wrong for even sending me over here to sell you the bullshit. He sent me on a bullshit suicidal mission, and for that I ain't really feeling him or his crew anymore." I answered in a disappointed tone. "I could tell that you had love for him Romello, but why? I explained how Tiger had taken me in after my first murder and that he was like family to me once upon a time. Yes, if any other Vato knew that you had the heart to kill, they would have taken you in too. It wasn't that he had love for you, it was so he could use you whenever he wanted too. That's not love, me and my brothers have love, and we protect each other.

The fact that you came by yourself that day should be proof to you that he didn't care what happened to you. That's what even made a check the Dope. Hector told me. Everything that he was saying made perfect sense and even though I hated hearing the truth, I had to accept it.

During our walk, I was all ears to what Hector had to say, "Look Romello, you seem like a cool kid, and for you to even come down here on your own to apologize and bearing gifts makes me respect you a person. Now the problem I have is with Tiger, and he has to pay. I lost a team member, and that's expected in this game but what asking you to do is to give me Tiger."Hector requested. I exhaled, "Hector with all dus respect, even though I'm not feeling Tiger or his brothers, and even though I know how foul he is but I just can't give him up like that. Then where is my loyalty? I'm trying to branch off from Tiger and leave him and his crew alone altogether. I'm waiting to be accepted to MSU right now, and I want to go legit."I told him.

We turned back around, heading back toward my truck. "That's good Esa', that real good your choosing school over the streets and respect your loyalty for him even though he is Slime-Ball me and my family are big on loyalty and respect but I have a feeling that you would change your mind about not giving his him up. Tiger will not be trying to hear that his prodigy quitting and has going to do whatever to keep you on his team... So with that being said, I appreciate you coming down here to make things right, and you're alright with me.

Call me if you need me or if you're ready to give Tiger up. Good luck with the college thing too."Hector told me, sticking his hand out for a handshake. I shook his hand and told him that I would call him if I ever changed my sins or needed his I hopped in my truck happy that I made things right with Hector but the as telling stayed bouncing through my mind. I don't think that Tiger would try and keep me in the streets rather than bein

?

school, would he?

Busy-n-Love

18

Madison's heart was broken, but there wasn't anything that I could do about it, and this wasn't the first time that I killed someone that she loved. All I could think to do was to make sure she never found out I was the one that killed Ebony. I began to actually believe that Madison really wanted to kill whoever was responsible for her best friend's murder because she often would ask me if I had heard anything yet. Every time I would tell her, "Not yet, Babe, but I'm still on it.". Sooner or later I was going have to tell her something, even if it was a lie.

The rain was coming down pretty hard while Madison and I stood under Our umbrella, holding each other's hands. Nothing would stop her from visiting the cemetery, especially any weather. We stood in front of Ebony's tombstone while Madison talked to her best friend as if she was present. Madison would update her about her and my life together, her busy week, and even some sorrority gossip, but what caught my attention was how she would promise that she was going to find her killer. When I took a look around the cemetery, I noticed Tiger's red Range Rover pulling behind my truck. I exhaled, not wanting to speak to Tiger, but it was time for me to stop dodging him and tell him what it really was. I kissed my baby on the cheek and told her to give me a few minutes.

I hoped in Tiger's passenger seat when he held his hand out for me to give him play, "Whasup Lil' Mello, what's good wit' you? I haven't seen or heard for you in bout' a month. Pit and Shark said that you haven't been by the house either.

?

You been laying up in that Lil' Maddy Pussy or something?. You been laying Up my calls and not calling me back. Shid, we starting to feel like we not family no more or something." Tiger said not wasting any time I wanted to laugh when that Nigga said "FAMILY",

""Shid man, it aint nothing like that. Just me and my girl been spending alot more time together and I'm getting ready to enroll in College to so I just been busy, that's all."I answered. Tiger nodded his head as if he understood, "Fasho,fasho. From what I hear, it sounds like your in love. I could feel all of that, but what about money? Ain't you ready to get back to the money? I got some jobs for you that would set your pockets straight." Tiger told me.

Knowing this had to be discussed, "Ummm about that, I'm actually pretty straight financially, and that's why I been wanting to talk to you. You've been like a big brother to me, and I appreciate everything that you had done for me from taking me in when I was young and paying me for my services. I've been accepted into Michigan State University and I will soon have a job. It's time for me to live a different life, you understand, right? I mean, your not mad or anything, are you?" I told him, followed by a question. He stored out of the window, and I could tell that a lot was going through his mind. I was his muscle. His killer and to lose an important person such as myself from his team would be a huge loss and a hard pill to swallow.

"Poor Lil' Maddy, she's over there standing in front of her best friends Tombstone not even knowing that her boyfriend was the killer, what a tragedy. You do want that to remain a secret, right?" Tiger asked, lookingover at me. I looked at him with a crazy but confused look and asking him what did he mean by that. Well you know what I mean....So be with shit! You're not done til' I say that your done I gotta; a lot of shit in the works right now and I fuckin' need you around to make sure that it gets handled. All that I dons for you and now your trying to quit?! Hell Nawl! Fuck Nawl! Now what I want you to do is come by the house tonight, and we gon'discuss what I need you to do, do I make myself clear?" Tiger said to me.

I couldn't believe what I been told; Tiger was threatening to tell Madison about me killing her best friend just because I wanted to quit. "Look at Lil Maddy; she looks like she really wants to know who is responsible for her best friend's murder. If I were you, I would make sure that I would be at the house tonight unless you want me to tell Lil' Maddy what the fuck you did. Now get the fuck outta' my truck you Disloyal Mutha'fucka!" Tiger told me. I stepped out of his truck at the same time; Madison was walking toward mines. When we hopped in my truck, I was still in shock as to what Tiger had just threatened me with. "What was so important that Tiger had to come and visit you here?" She asked.

"Huh? Oh, ummm, he was just telling me how he needed me to stop by tonight. I answered her. I pulled out of the cemetery mentally fucked up From Tiger and my conversation. "Hey Babe...So have you heard

⍰

anything about Ebony's Killer yet? I mean, I know you been with me everyday but I was just hoping you did, ya know?

"Nawl not yet but I think I'm getting warmer, just give me a couple more days and I'll be able to give you something," I told her.

I Can't Wait

19

I dropped Madison off at her father's while I headed back to my old meet up with Tiger and his Brothers. Earlier, when we talked through the cemetery, I could barely respond to Tiger's threats and comments, but after a couple of

hours passing, I was pissed to the max. This nigga Tiger wanted me to stick around so bad that he was willing to rat me out to my own girlfriend, and there was no telling who else he would have ratted me out too. He was breaking one of the most important street lows there was, and that was to never snitch under any circumstances. When I pulled up in front of my old house, I noticed that everybody was here, including Tiger's brothers. When I parked others. When I parked, I put my glock 9mm on my waist and stuck my swiss army knife in my socks. There was no telling what they would be on in the house, so it was better that I was prepared rather than been sorry. For a brief

?

moment, the thought to go in and killing everybody inside was crossing my mind, but I decided to wait it out and see exactly what it was that they wanted from me.

I walked into the house, and it was trashed like the Spot that they alway wanted it to be. Soon as I walked in, Pit stopped me and patted me down like I was a type of stranger. He removed my pistol from my waist and told me that it was for everybody's safety. Tiger was sitting on the couch, while Pit, and Shark went to sit down at the other couches. Muthafuckin! Lil' Mello, whasup Man? I heard you trynna' leave us and go chasing after Lil' Maddy, what's up with that? Didn't we treat you like family, and this his how you do us?" Shark asked, drinking from his bottle of liquor.

"Yea, yall treated me just like family but a nigga grown up now, and I'm just straight on this street shit! We pose to be like family, but yall want me to keep killing for yall, and that's not going to happen. That's why I'm here; I'm here to tell yall that I'm done with that shit." I answered, looking at all of them in their faces. The room grew silent, and I could tell that they all felt a bit guilty, as they should. Tiger stood to his feet, well yea I hear you and all I plan to let you gon' head and do yo' thang but...I got two more jobs

I need you to do first. Now if you don't do the jobs that I'm assigning to you, then I would simply tell yo' lil' girlfriend Maddy that your a hitman that's taken jobs such as her best friend and her brother. If, by chance, you think that she would not believe me, then I would have to use more drastic measures and tell the Detroit Homicide Division that I have a lead on multiple murders. I'm sure they would appreciate the tip." Tiger told me.

Tiger was using the murders he paid me to do to blackmail me. "You been planning this shit for the past three weeks, haven't you? You a Dirty Mutha'fucker!" I yelled at him. Tiger looked at his brothers then back at me when he started laughing, "Three weeks?! Nigga, why do you think I took you in? Gave you a house? A good Lifestyle? Cars, money, and jewelry? I been planning this against you since I first met you when you were a kid! I knew the day would come when you would try to leave, and that's why I been preparing. What? Why are you looking like that? Did you... Did you really think that we were family?! Ha, ha, Ha Lil' Mello. Haven't you learned anything from me? Always develop relationships with people so you could use them for something." Tiger said,

[?]

laughing and giving his brothers plays. Not wanting to risk Tiger ratting me out, "What's the fuckin' mission man?!" I asked in a pissed off tone submitting to his threats. Tiger nodded his head,

"I thought you would see it my way, you're kinda smart. I guess I could keep our lil secret to myself then...I'll be calling you in a couple of days to give you the details of the mission. Leave my sight, you fuckin' schoolboy!" Tiger told me. I mugged all of them before opening up the front door; Pit stood up, taking the clip out of my pistol and handing me back my gun. "I'm sure you have another clip in that nice truck that you have there. Get the fuck on!" He told me, pushing me out of the door. I left the house furious but had to pull myself together. I had to be smart, and most importantly, I had to be smarter than Tiger. I had to come up with a plan, but what would it be? I knew Tiger well enough to know that after I completed his missions that he would kill me, and I refused that to happen. I had two days to make something happen and to come up with a plan.

Bitter Sweet

20

On the long car ride back home, there were so many things that were running through my mind that I damn near forget that Madison was riding passenger. A lot must have been on her mind, also being that she was silent the whole car ride as well, and that was not like her. I looked over at Madison, and she was staring out of the passenger window. I reached over and placed my hand on her lap, "Baby, is everything okay?" We been riding for over thirty minutes, and you haven't said anything." I asked a bit concerned. She looked over at me with a slight grin on her face, "Huh? Oh, I'm okay. I just was thinking about somethings, about life, about us," She answered. I knew a deep conversation was on the way and of course, I fed into it and asked her what it was that she comes up with. A panicking type, sickness look shot across her face, and her cheeks quickly blew up like something was in her mouth. She pointed and tapped on the window, signaling for me to pull over. I pulled over to the side of the road, where she opened the door and puked across the grass. I hopped out of the truck

🔲

and ran over to her side, "Damn, ughh... You okay? What did you eat?" I asked, patting her on her back. When she finally pulled herself together, she stepped out of the truck, telling me that she had something to tell me.

Completely clueless as to what was going on, "Ummm, I'm twelve weeks pregnant Romello. I found out a couple of days ago." Madison told me with her voice, crackling. My mouth dropped and I was in a complete shock. I stood there looking Madison up and down, but her tears rolling down her face confused me. I stepped closer to her and put my arm around her, "What's wrong Baby? This is good news, right? Why the tears? I asked her. "It's just... It's just that we are so busy, your starting school, I'm in school and... I'm just a little scared. "Madison told me. I wiped the tear from her eyes, "Awww Baby, don't trip cuz' we got this. We gon' work it out, yea we both in school but we gon' be straight. This Baby is the best news that I heard in a long time and I'm proud and honored to create a new life with the woman that I am crazy in love with." I told her while looking into her eyes. Hearing that I was excited instead of disappointed put a smile on Madison's face, "I'm so happy to hear you say that....Oh my God, we're having a baby."

She said joyfully and jumping into my arms, kissing me. "And we will be the best parents we can be, I know it." I told her. A State Trooper pulled up behind my truck, asking if everything was okay. Everything's good officer, My girl just had a lil' pregnancy sickness that's all." I answered, helping Madison inside the truck. I jogged back around, jumping back into the driver's seat, feeling good. After all of the crazy things that have been going on in my life, it was about time that things seemed like it would get better. It was a bittersweet feeling because I was still involved in the streets, but it was sweat because Madison and I were being blessed with a child that was surely made from love. I was going to be the best Father ever.

Small Ass World

21

"What?! Get the fuck on! Nawl bro, swear? That's whasup!! We bout' to fuckin' celebrate! I ain't tryna' hear all that you don't smoke or drink shit!

This cause for a celebration! You fuckin having a Lil' one, Bro!" Killa Kam said as he went over to his mini-bar and poured a glass of Ace of Spade to bring over to the table with him. He handed me my glass, "This is to you being a not only a great Father but an even better Father then either one of us had and to your child living a good life...Salute," Killa Kam said as we both lifted our glasses for a toast. He drank from the bottle, and I sipped from my glass. Only because it was Killa Kam that I decided to take a sip. After sipping the nasty champagne, I shocked Killa Kam, even more, when I asked him to be my child's Godfather. He couldn't believe it and jumped up and down in excitamant; he to take a big gulp from his bottle just to calm himself down. He came over to me unable to resist hugging me, "Bro, it's an honor to be your child's Godfather, are you fuckin! kidding me?! I can't hold you up I hope its a girl so I could spoil her crazy!" Killa Kam said. "I don't care if it's a boy or a girl, just as long as it's a healthy baby," I told him.

Interrupting our baby talk, the doorbell rang, "Oh shit, I forgot my Eastside Nigga that be spending money with me was stopping by to check out that jewelry you sold me. I'm bout' to tax this nigga real quick." Killa Kam said before answering the door.

A big fat black nigga walked through Killa Kam's door, and when I saw him I almost clutched on the pistol that was on my hip. It was the same big fat and black nigga that I shot in the neck months ago. Killa Kam introduced us, and I couldn't help but notice the scar that was in the middle of his throat from the bullet wound. He stuck his hand out and we gave each other play, "You look familiar, do I know you from somewhere?" Jason asked me. I shook my head, answering no, when Killa Kam headed to the backroom, "Shid, yall both from the Eastside, but I don't know Jason. My nigga, right there is the Eastside Assassin, straight killa for Hire. You wouldn't want to know him." Killa Kam told him. This nigga Killa Kam was clearly drunk for telling this nigga my business, and he didn't even know me. "You gotta excuse my nigga here, he drunk, and It's not even 3 pm. I told Jason, Jason nodded his head but still was staring at me as if he was trying to remember where he knew me from. Killa Kam came from the backroom with a suitcase and opening it up on the table, telling him to come over and take a look. Before heading over to the table, Jason had asked me if I ever had braids, and I answered him. "Nawl he ain't never had no braids Nigga, That's my brother right there, and I know you don't know him. Now would you come on and take a look at this shit." Killa Kam said to him.

I stood to the side with my shirt raised just enough to draw my pistol if I needed to clutch on this fat nigga. I couldn't believe that this nigga Killa Kam knew this nigga enough to even invite him over to his house. The fat Nigga Jason Degan checking out all of the jewelry and the pieces that I sold Killa Kam, and all of it was still there. Jason stood there staring at all of his deceased Homeboy's jewelry, and I knew he knew it, "So how long you had all of this stuff? Where did you get it from?" Jason asked. Killa Kam told him that he was asking too many questions and if he wanted the pieces then he should hurry up and buy because we had things to do that's exactly what Jason did, he bought all of his deceased friend jewelry back.

We walked his fat black ass outside when we all exchanged plays on the porch. I pulled my shirt back down when I realized that wasn't anything about to go down. "Yo' Jason, that's a nice Benz Truck; you got there Boy." Killa Kam complimented the Benz while still sipping from the Ace of Spade bottle. Before heading over to his Benz, Jason turned around, "Fasho Man, it just draws to much-unwanted attention is what I don't like. I'm actually looking for a Charger that's triple black and that I could put some rims on it. Ya know, something I could be a lil low-key in." He replied. I off top knew what he was doing, and he thought that he was slick with his fishing techniques. "Oh yeah? My mans right here just had one exactly how you described the one that you want. I been on his ass telling him that he should sell it. I don't know if you could call it something that's considered Low-key because his shit been shot up and everything before." Killa Kam told him. Right at that moment Jason took a look at me and grinned, out of sight from Killa Kam I raised my shirt back up and purposely showing the pistol that was on my waist. It was official he knew who I was, he just hopped in his truck and pulled off. I then memorized his license plates, the time would come that we would have to deal with each other, but it wouldn't be in front of our mutual Friend....

Love Aint No Love

21

(LATER THAT NIGHT)

Madison asked me to drop her off at her father's house so she could help him while he was sick. When I turned down the block, I saw Tigers Brother Pit parked out in front of Manny's Club talking to him. I was sure that he was picking up the extortion money that Manny had to pay monthly that I use to once pick up for Tiger before I tried quitting. As we rode he stopped talking to Manny just so he could mug me through my tinted windows. Madison asked why he was looking at us crazy when I told her that he was being his same playful self. Telling Madison about the tension between Tiger and his brothers was not an option. There was no need to stress her because they were stressing me to stay in the streets and working for them.

After dropping Madison off, I headed down the block when I noticed Pit and Manny were no longer standing outside, and Shadow and his crew's cars were now parked out front, which meant that they were inside as well. Pit and Shadow's crew was like mixing oil and water together; there was guaranteed to be a problem inside the club because neither side could filter their slick comments toward each other. I pulled behind all of their cars and grabbed my extra clip out of the glove compartment before-hopping out to assist Pit. When I stepped out of the truck and headed inside the club I quickly had myself an epiphany.

Why was I about to help this nigga Pit? He was one of the niggas trying to keep me in the street life. He was laughing and high-fiving his brothers as they told me they only took me in and showed me love so they could mold me into their own killer. Then I began remembering times when they did look out for me and treated me like their younger brother. They could tell me they were caps just playing roles as far as treating me like family, but some things could not be acted. At time they treated me like one of their own, but the majority of the time, I did hate them. I needed to start coming up with a plan to defeat Tiger and his brothers so I could move on with my own life.

I stapped inside the club, and the loud sounds of moans, groans, screams, and begging were echoing over the loud sounds of an aluminum bat being hit against Pit's body. Manny stood in a corner scared to death while

Shadow and his crew were beating on Pit in the other corner. When they saw me step in, they all stood still and stared over at me, wondering what my reaction would be to them beating someone that I once called family. On the floor underneath Shadow and the crew was Pit, who was covered in blood, lumped and swollen up barely able to see out of his eyes. "Mello...Mello, help.me bro. Help me kill these niggas." Pit begged, barely able to speak. I began thinking of all his bullshit I was going through then I thought about any unborn child.

How could I live with myself letting somebody that I considered family to be killed "I never was here, yall hear me?" I said to Shadow and his crew. They all nodded their heads okay, this was the first time that Madison's brothers and I could ever be cordial about a situation that we were not trying to kill the other."Mello!! Romello lil' Mello, you gonn let them kill Me?! Mello!" Pit struggled, trying to yell at me. I turned back and headed out of the club's door allowing Shadow and his crew to continue to brutally beat Pit to death.

Right before the door closed behind me, I heard the bat go across his head, shutting him completely up. How could I live with myself, letting somebody I considered family to be killed? Like I have been living with myself after all of the murders I committed, just fine. Fuck Tiger and his family!!!!!

Chapter

22

(NEXT DAY)

I walked into my old house and Tiger and Shark were already there, I walked in on the end of their discussion when I caught them naming the places that their brother could have been. "I don't like this, I don't like this at all Tiger. His phone is never turned off or going straight to the voicemail. Something gotta be wrong. I'm telling you." Shark was saying in a worried tone. Tiger was his usual laidback self, "Stop tripping, don't panic...Pit probably just got fucked up and is laid up with some bitch at a Hotel somewhere. Call Manny lil fat ass again; Pit was supposed to go and pick up that forty thousand from him.' Tiger told his brother Shark. "Have you seen Pit or talked to him?" Tiger asked me with a straight face I looked at him and answered no.

"Aight then, on another note...So look, You know how much we hate Shadow and his lil' Crew and shit tight? Well, I know how imma' get them niggas and got the perfect tick. Since them, niggas been running around town, fucking up my money and trying to steal my clientele imma just fuck their money up, literally.

[?]

Shadow has a safe that has at least five bricks of heroin and save a couple of dollars in it, I need you to go and get it and bring it back to me."

Tiger told me. I looked at him like he was crazy, "So you want me to just waltz up in his place and hit his safe? C'Mon Man, How am I pose to do that I asked. Tiger grinned, "Shadow did wifed one of my old bitches who still got mad love for me, and she knows this combination. She gon' pop that bitch open for you, the only thing about it is that you would have to whoop the bitch ass when you're done so it could look like a real robbery and not staged. And that's it; your down one mission with one more to go." Tiger explained like it was easy.

After hearing the plan, it actually didn't sound too bad, I was so ready to be done with Tiger and his brother that I was willing to do anything to be officially done with them. The only thing that made me question this particular Like was how could I do this Lick and Tiger already threatened to rat me out to the police for the ones I already done. Tiger than assured me that he would only rat on me if he had to, and at the time he needed me more than ever. I agreed to do the lick, and when I asked him when the best time to hit Shadow's safe, he told me to go now in his neighborhood between us. "I need you to be on point and ready for her to text you. Hey, don't beat her up too bad, she is still, my bitch. Tiger sold with a light chuckle.....!

(1 am)

I sat in my Charger parked around the corner from Shadow's house and patiently waiting on his girlfriend to text me telling me that it was a go.

The disloyalty and betrayal she was willing to commit against her man for some money and some of Tiger's time still had me fucked up. She was going as far as getting beat up just to make sure that this lick didn't seem like it was staged. I didn't understand how any of it was worth it, I sat behind my wheel in all black everything with my wig on that had the dreads attached, my .45 on my lap, knives in my pockets and socks, and a mask to be put on. At the right time and phone in hand, waiting for the text message. A text had finally come through telling me that Shadow just left and for me to come on. I stepped out of my car, and behind I saw Shark's car parked a couple of houses down. I was pretty sure that his only reason for being here was because Tiger no longer trusted me and wanted to make sure that everything I took from Shadow's house was accounted for. He was taking all of the necessary precautions to get all of Shadow's Work.

Shark gave me a head nod before I handed over to Shadow's house. Since Shadow lived the next block over, I had to creep through e neighbors yard and jump over the gate to Shadow's backyard. I put my mask on and stopped at the side door where my girlfriend was already waiting for me. She opened the door, letting me in, "Ohhh shit, Boy, you scared the shit out of me. Why you got a mask on?" She asked. I told her that I didn't know her or trust her, Tiger or his brother, so I was cautious of my surroundings. She laughed and led me to the bedroom, where I assumed the safe was.

Shadow's Girl began putting in the combination to the safe, "Okay, before you beat me up, all I ask is that you don't knock out any of my tenth, Okay? Deal?" She asked, singing the Safols door open. I looked inside the safe and seen Rucks of money and stacked up Bricks. I looked at her and hit her with the hardest punch to the fast without warning. I like she was a Man. I tried to I literally-knock out every tooth that was in her mouth. When she fell back onto the bed, I jumped on top of her and began beating her into a pulp and releasing my anger.

My gloves were covered in blood, and she could barely even move. I picked up her cell phone and began deleting all text messages sent to me. I threw her phone on the bed and began unloading the safe into a pillowcase. It was one hundred and fifteen dollars and eight bricks of heroin. I put all of the money in a separate pillowcase as well as four of the bricks. This half was going to be mine and never reported to Tiger. I then checked over the bedroom, making sure that I covered my steps before I left the house, leaving the girlfriend in a puddle of her own blood. Soon as I stepped outside I looked for a good place to stash my pillowcase then I jumped back over the gate and through the neighbors yard stashing in a neighbors bushes.

I took my mask off as I headed to my car, and before I know it, Shark was pulling up beside me to take the bag of stuff that I just took from Shadow's Safe. He hopped out of his car, "I'll take that..Good job, fucker, is this everything?" He asked me as he looked inside the bag. When I answered yes, he looked at me funny and began patting me down just in case I was lying. "Where is the money that was supposed to be in the safe?" Shark asked. I shrugged my shoulders, I guess it wasn't because I grabbed everything that was in there." I answered. Sherk gave me a funny look, "Yea aight then." he said before hopping in his truck and pulling I hopped in my truck and hit a couple of corners making sure that I want I wasn't being followed and when I saw that I wasn't doubled back to where I parked before hitting the lick and went back for the pillowcase that held my hundred and fifteen thousand dollars and four bricks of heroin. I didn't know what that nigga Tiger was thinking my car with a grin on my face, I didn't know what that Nigga Tiger was inking, but I was no longer part of his team, and therefore I was never working for free. I was getting mines off the top...

Casulaties of War

22

I had already begun school, and it was a lot harder than I had expected to attend a good college such as MSU, I had to focus my attention on my work and with that was going on in my life that was very hard.

Between Madison being pregnant with my little girl and all the stuff that was going on in the streets, I just couldn't be totally committed like treats. Then I had to deal with a very hormonal girlfriend who wanted to leave couldn't be totally committed like I should have been. Then I had to deal with a very hormonal pregnant girlfriend who wanted me to leave the streets alone one minute then she wanted me to find out who killed her best friend, Ebony. I was going through a lot and needed to handle all of the issues one by one and accordingly.

After one of my classes, I headed down the school's hallways when Madison caught up to me with a kiss. She was already showing, so she now walked with a waddle. Walking beside me with her backpack on her back and her purse in hand. "Hey, babes, have you heard all of the crazy news that is going on in the neighborhood? She asked.

I answered no and asked her how she was still hearing what was going on in the hood being that we were a million miles away from Detroit. She told me that her father heard everything that would go on in the hood, and the talk of the hood was that the police found Pit's body in the Detroit River beaten to death. She also heard that Shadow's girlfriend's house was broken into, and he was robbed, and his girlfriends were left beaten into a coma. "My daddy told me that the niggas In the hood are tripping and Tiger and his brother has a hundred thousand dollars reward on any information," Madison told me.

I acted surprised by the news that she had just told me but was far from it, of course, I was only waiting for everybody else to get the latest gossip, I already know of it. It sounded like the hood was going crazy. Tiger and his crew were thirsty with the reward money, niggas in the hood we choosing sides, and shit was only going to get more real by the time it was all over with. This was all apart of my plan, and I felt good knowing that it was all working out.

"Are you okay, though? Madison asked with concern. I told her that I was okay and that since all of my classes are done for the day that I would see her a little later. She agreed, we told each other that we loved the other went our separate ways.

As I walked through the school's parking lot, my phone had rung, it was from an unknown number. When I answered, I was surprised it was Shadow. He asked me if we could meet up and when I told him I was two hours away from Detroit, he said that it was even better than I wasn't. For a nigga, especially a hood nigga, to leave the city just to have a talk with somebody meant that it was really serious. Shid, if I had taken a loss for a hundred and fifteen thousand dollars and eight bricks of heroin, I would be willing to travel my ass as well. I didn't care what anybody said, taking a loss like that would guarantee hurt someone's pocket. It would be even worse if Shadow was fronted and being that he had just come home that was most definitely a possibility...

I sat in a parking lot of seven-eleven waiting on Shadow to pull up, and I couldn't even lie; I was a bit nervous wondering what it was that he wanted to talk to me about. I sat there with my pistol on my top, and under my shirt when he had finally pulled up and beside me in a Camaro. He hopped out his car right into the passenger seat of my truck, his hand out for play. With the loss that he took, he was moving, floating, and grinning as if everything was just fine.

He was still nicely dressed, jewelry on, and looking like money regardless as to what reality actually was. If I was in his shoes, I'm pretty sure that I would be riding around with my pistol trying to kill whoever I thought was responsible.

"So what do I us this visit from the Big Dog Shadow?

You traveled mighty". I asked him with one hand under my shirt with my finger on the trigger. "Whos, relax Killer, this is a somewhat friendly visit. For starters, I wanna tell you I appreciate you for keeping that situation with Pit down at Manny's place to yourself. That was real, maybe even a little hard for you to do. The only reason you let it happen was because Tiger and his brothers must have shitted on you. Like I told you, they would." Shadow said, hitting it right on the nose. My silence had spoken for Itself, "My house was broken into about a week ago, and one hundred and twenty thousand dollars plus ten bricks of heroin was taken from my safe and made to look like my bitch was forced to open it, but I'm far from stupid. I know fasho that wasn't the case. "Shadow told me.

Even though he boosted up the limit of things taken from his safe, I was curious to know what he meant by his statement. "Whatchu' means you know fasha that wasn't the case? I asked. He chuckled, " My bitch knew my combination and that was my first mistake, but when I found her phone, all of her text messages were erased, but I found Tiger and Sharks number in her phonebook. I'm sure they had their hands in what happened. I just know it." Shadow said so confident in what he figured happened. I sat there, just nodding my head, still silent. "Lil' Mello, I need to know the truth... Did you know about this lick, and if not, what do you know about it now? I know the streets are talking." Shadow asked me.

I told Shadow that Tiger and his Brothers had been

stopped discussing around me since I told them that I wanted out of the crew. I told Shadow that the only thing that I did know was that Tiger and Shark goes to this girlfriend in the hospital often. "That's all I know... Damn, sorry about yo girl income, though." I told him sounding like I was sincere. He laughed, "That ain't my bitch no more. She slipped into a coma, and I hope that she slips into death so I could save money on paying a hitman to kill her. Fuck that bitch." Shadow said getting angry just thinking about his disloyal ex-friend.

Shadow calmed himself down by taking a deep breath, "So look, I have an offer for you. I have a hundred thousand dollars on any info that leads me into my house. I have a feeling that it was Tiger and his brother doing, but I need to be sure. I'm offering you two hundred thousand dollars to set Shark up for me so that I could kill somebody who I didn't even fuck with anymore was a no-brainer.

I would have done it for cheaper, but I was just waiting for the right time. At the same time, I know how to play situations such as this. I told Shadow that I would have to think about and get back at him with an answer. He smiled at my answer, and I was pretty sure that he knew that I would accept the mission. Shadow reached in his pocket and pulled out a stack of money the long way, "Well here is a hundred thousand dollars right here. I will give you the other half the moment you deliver." I'll see you soon, Killa. Shadow told me before hopping out my truck and into his car.

Before we both pulled off from the parking lot, Shadow

rolled down his window signal for me to do the same. "Oh yea, I almost forgot. Catch! He told me before tossing over a brown paper bag into my true and pulling off. I opened the bag head and poured the item into my lap, It was Pit's diamond chain.

Almost Ready

23

I stood in my studio apartment wearing a Polo jogging fit, my gold Jesus chain, and wheat Timberland boots on my feet while standing over my bed with the A-R assault rifle laying beside the luggage bag full of my money and jewelry. It wasn't often that I would do an inventory check, but with all of the money I been tucking, making, and paying off tabs to the Mexicans, it needed to be done. Plus, I wanted to stash the majority of my possessions somewhere safe because it wasn't smart to keep everything in one place. Even though I hated Tiger's guts, I did learn some valuable lessons from him. I had four hundred and fifty-seven thousand dollars, four bricks of heroin and jewelry box full of some of the iciest jewels I ever seen. In another big luggage bag, I had all of my murdering supplies that included my masks, wigs, and uniforms. Madison walked into the apartment when I closed the luggage that held all of my murdering supplies quickly. She walked toward me, laughing at my poor effort to try and hide something before she came in.

"Babe, what are you doing in here with that sneaky look on your face? What is all this stuff you got on your bed? I Just cleaned..." Madison was saying until she stepped close enough and actually seen what one of the luggage actually contained. The look on her face was evident that she never seen so much money and jewelry in her life. "Romollo.... What is this? Either you done robbed a bank or you haven't just been running "ERRANDS' for Tiger. What is going on?" She asked me.

There was no easy way to explain that I was a hitman so I was completely frozen in what to say. I walked up to Madison placing my hands on both of her hips, "Baby.. You know that I love you dearly and always been honest with you, but. It doesn't even matter what I do because I don't do it anymore, and my days in the streets are very, very close to being done. This money is for us. For our daughter's future, so she could have a better life than we ever did. I need you to trust me and know that I would never jeopardize you or our daughter's safety, okay? Our family would soon be able to live peacefully very soon." I told her as I pulled her in closer to give her a warm and comfortable hug.

Madison sat on the bed, looking like she had just seen a ghost, When? exactly will you be done in the streets because seeing this much money scares me." She asked. I reached in the luggage of money and took a hundred thousand of it out and zipped it up. "No exact date, but very soon. I'm taking all of this stuff going to stash it for a rainy day. Just know that we set, our family is set." I answered her as I carried one of the luggage bags to the front door.

Madison tried picking up the other luggage bag when all of my costumes, masks, wigs, and a couple of guns fall out. I rushed over, trying to pick up as much as I could hoping that she didn't see much, but that was

?

impossible. "What the fuck is all of this shit Romello?" She asked, picking up the wig that had braids attached to it. I snatched it away from her and began stuffing it all back into the luggage bag it fell from. "This is just some stupid shit that Tiger wanted me to deliver to somebody. Aight Baby. I gotta' go. Love you, bye!" I said, moving all of the bags of luggage out of the apartment.

After loading my truck up, I sat there not only sick that Madison seen all that she picked up the same wig that I killed her best friend in. The same braids with the same fitted cap Ebony described to her as the description of the killer that killed Trey and her friend. "Could she?? Could she put two and two together?" I asked myself...

Homework

24

After stashing my luggage in a secure and safe place. I pulled out my computer and used the same computer program that I used to find out where Madison's best friend Ebony lived at. It was time for me to find out where it was that Jason, who I shot in the neck, lived at before he tried to ride on me and caught me slipping first. I know from our eye contact that we both came up with the solution that the other had to die. I typed in his license plate number that I had memorized and address and government name popped up instantly. Most niggas that was in the streets never put cars in their name, but luckily he did, which allowed me to find out exactly where he was listed as a residential. It was time for me to pay this nigga a visit....

(1 pm)

I pulled up a couple of houses down from the address that his car was listed too, and now I just wanted to make sure that he still lived here or visited this address, so I wouldn't be trying to kill him at the wrong house. I was officially on a stake-out just waiting and hoping that he would just pull up, proving that he actually lived here. I sat parked down the street from the house for seven hours straight, waiting for him to show up and just when I was ready to give up for the day my time had paid off.

The same Mercedes Benz Truck that he pulled up to

?

Killa Kam's house pulled up in the driveway to the address that I had him listed under. He went in and spent over an hour inside before leaving again, then he pulled back up to the house three hours later and was in for the night. After a long day of staking out, it was official that this was where Jason lived, and when the time was right, I was going to kill him in that exact house. "Gotchu' now nigga!" I said as I pulled away with a devious grin on my face....

Step One

25

I called Tiger and Shark telling them to meet me at the house because I had important news to tell them. Which they both agreed to do. Earlier today was Pit's funeral, so I knew that they were both emotional over the loss of their brother. At this time, any news was considered important news, and they could not afford to miss out on the information. They both pull up at the same time in separate cars and hopping out wearing suits. When I looked at Shark, I could tell that he was taking the lost the hardest; he and Pit were the closest. If Shark had any clue at all as to who was responsible for his brother's death, I knew for sure that he would be ready to ride with no questions asked. Tiger was upset, but he was good at masking his emotions, he always was. I never saw Tiger get emotional under any circumstances.

When I walked into the house, Shark went straight for the refrigerator to grab some cold alcohol so he could numb the pain that he was enduring."So what's the news that was so important that you needed to tell us right away?" Tiger asked me before flopping on the couch and untieing his tie. I sat across from him, "Now, even though yall niggas already admitted to shitting on me and telling me that yall never considered me like family. I still could not let Pit's murderer slip away. I know who It was that killed it, and they been around

?

the city bragging. I got all of his info. His name and address are the most important, though." I told them. The looks on both of their faces looked like they had just seen a ghost.

Shark jumped up, "Who did it?! Where they at?! I'm ready right fuckin' now! I'm bout' to go and get the guns so we could ride!" he said hyped and ready to avenge his brother's murder. "Calm down, relax; we have to make sure this information is accurate first. How did you find this out, Lil' Mallo? Who is this nigga that killed my Lil' brother, and why?" Tiger asked me. "Why do it fuckin' matter, Tiger? Lil' Mello is telling is he done his fuckin' homework and found out who killed our brother, and you want to ask a stupid question instead of fucking riding? Let's go and kill this nigga." Shark yelled at Tiger.

Tiger exhaled, knowing that his brother was very emotional. " We have to be logical about this, Shark. We have to do things the right way. We have that big deal coming up, and the thing we need is for one of us to end up dead or in jail because we were moving so fast." Tiger explained to his brother. Shark then stood in front of Tiger."You wanna' prolong avenging our brother for some fuckin' deal that's coming up is what you're telling me? Fuck tat deal and fuck you too! With or without you, I'm riding on whoever this nigga is," he yelled at his brother before stomping out of his house.

The room was silent, with only Tiger and Myself in it. I could tell that Tiger was under a lot of stress and had a lot on his mind. I apologized for bringing the information to them, "I just thought that yall would wanna handle the situation personally." I told Tiger. Tiger got up and poured himself a drink, "Look, I know you wanna go and do yo own thang, and truthfully commend you for it. Regardless of what I said before, you were always like family to me. After we do this deal that I got coming up in the next couple of weeks, Imma' let you go and do yo own thang. I won't be telling anybody none of the things that you've done in the past or nothing to that nature. I just need you to look after my brother for me; he's all I got.

Don't give that nigga the address to the nigga that did killed our brother until the deal is done, okay? Tiger asked me. None of the shit he was saying I believed, he just wanted me to watch out for his brother so that he doesn't end up dead as well. I decided to play the same game that he was playing, and I looked his direction in his face telling him that I would not give his brother the address to the killer's house. I gave him a play and left.

Killing Two Birds/ One Stone

26

(The next night at 11pm)

⸮

Tonight was the night that Shark and I were going to avenge his brother's death. This is the first time ever took anybody with me to kill, but this particular time wasn't an issue. He was dressed in his all black apparel, had his own gun and masks, so he was ready to kill. We sat seven houses down from where Pit alleged Killer lived; now we were just playing the waiting game for him to come home. "So who is this nigga, and why did he kill my brother? Shark asked me. I told him that all I heard was that Shadow had something to do with it. Soon as he heard that Shadow had his hands in it, he automatically got even madder. "Once we handle this, Imma' handle that Bitch Ass Nigga Shadow! Shark promised.

(1:30 am)

Shark's phone vibrated, it was his brother Tiger, but Shark sent him to the voicemail. Tiger knew his brother well, and he knew that he was very emotional as far as avenging their brother's death. "Man, this nigga Tiger been on my ass!

Nawl nigga I'm taking care of the business your pose' to be handling!" He said to his phone before putting it back in his pocket. I tapped Sharks arm getting his attention.

There he go, that's him. That's him right there!"

I said anxiously. "Bet, let's run up on him and kill him soon as he gets out the car."

Shark suggested. "Nawl Man, that's not how we gon' do it. We gon' do it right, just hold on Dog, we gon' get him." I assured the eager Shark.

We waited for the guy to get out of the Benz Truck and take his female friend inside of his house. After a few minutes, we crept out the car and up toward the house

with mask on and guns ready. I peeked through the living room window where I saw him on the couch, receiving oral sex from the woman he had taken in with him. I grinned when I saw how easy this would be, I looked around his front yard for anything that could be useful, and I found a big ass wrench.

I picked it up and signaled for Shark to stand beside the front door while I prepared to kick it open. "Nigga we got guns, what the fuck you need that big ass wrench for? Shark whispered. Ignoring his question, I stepped back and ran to kick the door open.

Kicking the door open the first time was successful, and we both ran inside. I cocked my arm back before slapping it across his mouth with it. The girl that was giving him oral sex sat there on her knees, screaming at the top of her lungs until the bullet from Shark's gun entered through her forehead, causing her body to flop on the floor. The nigga I just slapped with the wrench across his mouth was rolling around on the floor. Moaning from the pain with his pants still down at his ankles. I shut the front door back closed, and Shark walked up to him, removing his mask to look his brother's assassin in the face, "Damn Dog, look like you

⁉

broke his jaw! Now I ain't gon' be able to get any response from this nigga!" Shark said, upset that his questions couldn't be answered.

I just shrugged my shoulders like it was a mistake, but indeed it wasn't. I didn't want him to be able to speak at all; my plan would have backfired. Shark sat him back up on the couch after pulling his pants back up and began beating the guy ass while asking him at the same time why did he kill his brother. I sat back on the other couch, watching Shark wear himself out while I removed my mask as well. Shark hit him with a hit so hard it made the guys head fall back to the floor, and when he helped him back up on the couch, the guy had seen my face for the first time. When he saw me, his eyes grew big, and the anger was written all over his face. He began breathing harder and mumbling, attempting to talk but still was unable to. Shark saw the look that the guy was giving me, "Ohhh, he acts like he fuckin' knows you Lil' Mello. What's his name, by the way?" Shark asked me. I sat there staring the guy in his face with a grin, "His name is Jason, he knows me because I killed one of his mans and now he's probably sick that I found out he killed yo' brother for Shadow." I answered.

Shark took his time with the brutal beating that he was putting on Jason, and I was loving every bit of it. I had time to send out a couple of text messages to, and it was only a matter of time before shit got more real than what Shark had expected. After about thirty minutes passed, I took a peek out of the front of the window of

Jason's house, and there were two cars pulling up. Shark was in a completely different zone while he beat Jason down. Beside me was Shark's pistol that he sat down, and I smoothly picked it up, tucking it without him noticing what I did. I stood to my feet and walked over to the kitchen entrance for a better view of the beating that was about to take place.

The front door opened while Shark was stomping Jason's lifeless body, and when he turned around and seen Shadow and his crew entering the house, his face dropped. He quickly dove over the couch where his pistol once was and calling my name at the same time. He immediately noticed that his pistol wasn't in the same place, and I was now standing out of the way. Right at that moment, he began to put two and two together, realizing that he had been set up. Shadow's crew rushed Shark and began beating his ass until he started looking like the dead nigga Jason.

Shadow and I stood back watching the brutal beating Shark was taking, and even after all the stabbings and being whooped with a pistol, Shark was talking shit. I always knew that Shark was a mad man, but this was clear proof that he was crazy. He was getting beat to the fullest, and all while taking it; he was cussing both Shadow and Myself out. I knew that he was sick that I set it up for him to kill somebody than to have him killed afterward.

Shadow told his crew to sit Shark up and to hold him up while he kneeled in front of him, "You and your brother's thought yall could just rob my place, beat my bitch up, and I wasn't gon' find out?! Now, look at you, pathetic!!

Shadow said to him. Remaining the tough nigga that he was and always been, he spit out a mouth full of blood in Shadow's face. "Fuck you and yo' fat ass bitch! My brother gon' use yo bricks to pay and have all of yall killed! Especially that bitch ass disloyal nigga back there!" Shark threatened. Shadow stepped back, wiping the blood from his face, "Well, that maybe, but we gon' stay here all night until you tell me where my work is stashed at. If you don't

tell, I can stay here all night enjoying watching you be beat to death. Starting now!" Shadow told him while his crew returned back, beating Shark. ...

Another thirty minutes passed and Shark still hadn't told where Tiger held all of Shadow's work. Truth be told, I was surprised that he was still alive. He had been beaten worse than what he did to Jason. Both of his eyes were swollen shut, his nose looked broken, and his face was covered in blood. Growing tired of Shark's silence, Shadow got up and booted Shark directly in his face, "Where is my shit, and I'll let you live!" Shadow yelled at him.

Barely conscience from his beating, Shark laughed while spitting up more blood, "My brother. . He gon' kill yall! I ain't telling you shit!" Shark tough-ass told him. Shadow walked back over to me, reaching in his pockets, handing me a stack of money the long way, "This shit is gon' take a lil' longer than I expected, this is the rest of your money. Gon' head and get outta' here, and we gon' take this nigga with us." Shadow told me. I stood up, reaching in my pocket and pulled out Pit's chain; I want him to be found with his brother's chain." I handed it to Shadow. We gave each other a play as he spoke. "Hey, the offer still stands for you to join my team. We taking over out here." Shadow told me. I grinned and told him I was just about done with the streets now. He nodded his head and congratulated me. Before I stepped out of the house, I heard Shadow tell his crew to strip Shark down naked, "We bout' to make him scream since he won't talk, hand me that broom over there." Shadow told them.

During my drive to my woman, I was all smiles and feeling like a slave that could see the end of the Tunnel. "Two down, one to go," I said to myself. Now I just had to come up with a plan to shake away from Tiger. It had to been well planned and unpredictable; all I knew was that I wanted him dead with his brothers....

Shit Has Changed

27

(TWO WEEKS LATER)

Leaving Madison's doctor's appointment, she asked me to take her to the city so she could visit her father, so I took her to the old neighborhood. Soon as I turned the corner, I could tell that so much had changed since the last time I stopped by. When we rode past Manny's club, I saw Dime doing the same one-two step I use to have to do when I was picking up the monthly squeeze, payments for Tiger now he was doing it. Riding through the hood I noticed the Dope Spots that use to be run by Tiger were now under new management. It looked liked Madison's brothers were running a few of them being that Shadow had taken the streets over. When I pulled up to Madison's house, I saw Shadow cruising down the block in a brand new Mercedes-Benz smoking a blunt and throwing up the deuces to me.

The neighborhood had done a complete 360, and I could tell that Shadow was flooding the blocks the same way Tiger use too. The beef I once had with Madison's brothers had no longer existed. We were now on speaking terms, gave each other plays and all. Ever since, I gave Shadow both Tiger brothers that helped him control the hood. These days Man-Man and Stone were seeing more money than they ever had seen with all the changes that been going on.....

Need You

28

I got an unexpected call from Tiger who didn't sound like himself, he asked, me to come holler at him at the house that I use to live in I told him that I was on my way, but really I just wanted to know where was his mind was at since one of his brothers was found dead a couple of weeks ago and his other brother Shark was still missing. I haven't talked to Tiger since the first couple of days after Shark disappeared, and he called me asking if I seen or heard from him. I told him that I haven't seen or talked to him since the time that I told both of them I knew who it was that killed their brother Pit. With a brother being dead and another one missing, I could only imagine how crazy he was when he began to lose his businesses to the competition.

(7 pm)

I walked into my old house, where I seen Tiger sitting at the kitchen table drinking liquor from the bottle and smoking a big blunt to the face. He was going back and forth between both substances, and I never seen Tiger go so hard since I knew him. "Tiger... Whasup Dog, you aight? What's going on with you?" I asked, looking around at the trashed house. "They found him; they found my brother Shark's body. He was found raped with a broomstick, stabbed up, pistol-whipped, and badly beaten... They burned my brother alive in a burning house." Tiger told me with his voice crackling from a broken heart. Hearing he was dead was not a surprise, but hearing all of the details was. I couldn't believe Shadow and his crew were torching people like that. "Damn Dog... who you think did it?" I asked, sounding concerned. He gulped from his bottle, "C'Mon man; It's the same niggas that killed Pit, took the hood

clientele from me and been wanting to take me outta the picture since that bitch came from prison! It's gotta be Shadow and his crew! It only makes sense!" Tiger yelled while pulling out a bag of cocaine, and pouring it on the top of the table before taking a big snort from. Tiger was at an all-time new level of stress because the same cocaine that we use to sell was the same that he was now snorting. He then chased the cocaine down with his bottle of Ciroc'.

That was when I had to step in and calm him down. Yes, I wanted to see Tiger's life crumble, but going the route he was going, he would kill himself, and I couldn't allow that to happen. If anything, I wanted to be the one to finish him off.

Tiger stood up stumblings and snatching his pistol from his waistband, aiming it at the ceiling, "I'll kill them Mutha'fucka! All of them! He yelled. I stepped back, ducking and dodging his pistol being waved around the room. I asked him to calm down and assured him that I would help him find whoever it was responsible for killing his brothers. "We just have to make sho' it was Shadow and his crew that did it first before we started a war with them, feel me?" I told him. Tiger put his gun

☐

down and agreed that I was right. He was sure that he would find proof that led Shadows and his crew as being his brother's killers. Finally, Tigers had calmed down, walking over the couches and flopped down.

"I have a big deal going on in the next couple of days with my outta' town niggas, my brothers were supposed to secure me while we handled business, but since they no longer here.. I need you Lil' Mellow. I swear to you that it won't ask you to do another mission for me. You could move on, and you would never hear from me again, and that's my word. I just need this million dollar deal to go down and shid, even I might jump out of this street life." Tiger told me. When I heard a million-dollar deal would be occurring, I was all ears "A million dollars, huh? And all I have to do is secure you? I asked him.

Tiger saw that I was interested, and I was amazed how it was like he was no longer intoxicated. I guess talking about a million-dollar deal would sober anybody up "Yes, a million dollars, all you have to do is watch my back while I take care of these outta town niggas. They think I'm selling them twenty bricks, lil did they know...I got eight of them, by the time they realize, I would already have the strap to their faces and laying them down so we could get out there. Boom! We outta there with a million-dollars. Them niggas wouldn't know what hit them. They some Ole'rich ass, blow millions on cars, clothes and businessese type of niggas. Trust me; It's gon' be easy." Tiger explained. I nodded my head, "And outta' free million dollars that you bout to get what do I get?" I asked. Tiger grinned, 'You get two hundred thousand of it...Whasup, you in or not?" Tiger asked, needing an answer.

I sat there thinking about the two hundred thousand that I would make and how it would be a good way to retire from the street life. Tiger never handled his business sloppy, so I knew if he said that the lick would be easy, then exactly what it was, "Lil' Mello, I need you, Lil' Bro!" Tiger told me badly, wanting me to answer yes. I then exhaled, "Aight Man, I'll go wit you, two hundred thousand dollars, right?". I answered and asked a question making sure that I understood the terms. Tigers got excited "Yes! Two hundred thousand dollars, my nigga! I'm telling you dog; I need this million dollars. It's gon'be just enough," Tiger replied.

After Tiger calmed himself down, he picked his bottle of liquor back up only to find it now, empty. "Damn! I need to get outta here and put myself around some women or something! Let's go out and hit the town one more time before we hit this lick. C'mon Bro, fuck wit' me."Tiger suggested. "Mmm, I don't really feel like.." I was saying before he cut me off. "C'mon bro, I ain't got no brothers no more to ride out wit' me. You all I got, man, fuck wit me," he asked with a needy type of voice. I looked at the time on my watch, Mmmm, where you trynna go?" I asked. He suggested we hit the all-white party that was downtown. He grabbed his car keys "I'm bout to run to the crib so I could get dressed, and you had to go and do the same thing. We bout to have fun tonight; Lord knows I need it." Tiger said as he headed but of the house. I told him I was going to get dressed and that I would meet him there.

Going to the White Party with Tiger was the least that I could do for him. It would be our last time ever going out together again. The difference between this time and any other time is I wasn't going as his security this time but as a friend. A moment like this is what I always was waiting on, but it was just a shame that both of his brothers had to be killed before it could happen....

White Party

29

19

(LATER THAT NIGHT)

The White Party in Detroit was not just a regular hood event; it was a monthly event that would bring the whole city out, literally. Anybody that was somebody was in attendance from NBA, and NFL Players to some of the hottest rappers, video vixens/models, and even a few actors would show up. Of course, some of the biggest dope boys and the baddest bitches would be there. It was rare that I would go out and have myself a good time, but the way how things had been going lately, I felt like it was a celebration to being at the end of my street lifestyle, which was a reason to celebrate. For the first time in a long time, I was happy with where my life was going. The fact that Tiger and my business was almost over felt good. I was eager to moving on and starting my family with Madison. This night of celebration would be a night to remember.

xxx

Tiger and I mobbed through the party fresh to death and shining like hood celebrities we were. We took a seat at the V.I.P. Booth that we had a reserved when we saw Shadow and his crew across the room in their V.I.P booth as well. They were having themselves a ball. They had numerous amounts of bottles of liquor on their table, they were surrounded by some of the baddest bitches, and they were looking like the stars that Shadow promised me that they would soon be. The entire crew was standing over there icy as they should be; they were running all of Tiger's old businesses, so they had the right to party how they were partying. When I looked over at Tiger, who was sitting beside me, I swear I saw fire burning in his eyes filled with hatred toward Shadow and his entire crew.

When Shadow see us from across the room he made his way through the party traffic to come and speak, I whispered to Tigar to keep his cool and be smooth when he arrived. Tiger just sat there with the toughest mug on his face as Shadow greeted me with a play. "Whatup doe Lil' Mello? Tiger? I know what your doing here Lil' Mello because this event is for ballers but what you doing here Tiger? I don't think you have enough money to be here." Shadow chuckled after the slick comment, he just said. Tiger played the same game, "I don't know why you thought I didn't, shid..I'.m straight after pro'ing up from the free bricks I got not to long ago." He replied, referring to the bricks taken from Shadow's safe. Shadow's crew then walked over, "Oh yea? Well, I guess you could afford to get in but... Where is your brothers at? I don't see them, will they be coming in later or something?" Shadow shot back with the low blow. With a quick comeback, "They won't be able to make it, but will your girl? Or do she still need some rest?"

Not able to keep his cool any longer, Shadow tried getting at Tiger when his crew stopped him and held him back. The entire party's eyes were on us, and Shadow's crew pulled him all the way back to their booth.

"Could you believe that hoe-ass nigga?! He brought up my brothers?! He thinks this shit is a game Tiger said full of anger .The waitress came over to our booth, asking us was there anything that she could get us. Tiger told her to bring us ten bottles of Ace of Spade, "Imma' shows that niggas what his money could do."Tiger said wanting to prove that he wasn't broke.

Tiger and Shadow held a stunting contest in who could order the most bottles, and they both had so many bottles that they began to pass them out to random females around the club.what made Tiger mad is: how Shadow was able to buy bottles and then send over ten more bottles to our booth with a note that read, COURTESY OF UR SPOTZ THAT'S MY SPOT NOW! When Tiger read that small note his eyes were redder then what I would assume the devil's eyes looked like.

"I'm killing that nigga, I swear to God! Oh yea, and when did yall get so cool that he comes over and gives you plays and shit? What's that about?" He asked me. I shrugged my shoulders acting clueless, "Shid, I be down in the hood taking Madison to her old mans house all the time and he just started speaking whenever he saw me. He ain't my nigga or nothing, but he respects a nigga. Madison's brothers even been cool with me and speaking on a regular." I answered. Tiger gave me a look as if he questioned my answer, Just be careful fuckin' with them niggas, I got a feeling they on some bullshit! Tiger told me.

"Is that my nigga?! Mello?! Whasup Boy?!" Killa Kam yelled, coming from across the room. I squinted my eyes and couldn't do anything but smile when I seen my best friend Killa Kam with his uncles behind him. I turned to my right a where Tiger reminded him who Kille Kam was. The look on Tigers' face was a look of confusion. Killa Kam and his two uncles seen Tiger standing beside me their eyes grew wide, and a grin spread across their faces, "Damn, Whasup Tiger? I guess we seeing each other now and in the next couple of days, huh?" Killa Kam's uncle Ace said as he gave Tiger a play. Now I was confused about how they knew Tiger.

⁐

"Umm Ace, body, How yall know Tiger?"I asked them. Tiger? Yea, we fuck wit' Tiger and been fucking wit' him for a long time. We do a lot of business together whenever we visit the city. Tiger, we didn't know you knew nephew here, Lil' Mello." Body said to Tiger and me.

"Awww yea, Lil' Mello here is my Lil' Bro. I didn't know that yall knew each other. That's crazy!" Tiger replied.

Killa Kam and I had shocking looks on our faces how everybody had already knew each other. That's when It popped in my head that this was the lick that Tiger been talking about was the BIG DEAL. Uncle Body was the rich ass fresh niggas that Tiger had planned on robbing. I looked over at Tiger, and he didn't even want to look me in the face"'Aight fellas tt's been fun, but it's time for me to get up outta here, I done had to much to drink.Lil Mello I'll call you. Aces and Body I'll see yáll in the next couple of days. I'm out."Tiger said before giving all of us a play and boy walking away. Killa Kam and his uncles wondered why the sudden departure from Tiger, but I had an idea why.

I excused myself from them and went to catch up with Tiger before he made it out the door, "Please tell me they are not the ones you were planning on robbing Tiger?!" I asked.

His silence and looking away was a good enough answer, "No! No! You cant do it! They are my people! Killa Kam is my friend! I can't let you do that. No! They are my fam !" I told Tiger, meaning every word I was saying.

With a straight face and showing absolutely no emotion regarding the topic, "Aight, okay. We won't rob them then. I'm just going to have to find another lick to hit." Tiger said, then turning to walk away from me. As I watched him walk away I just shook my head, I knew Tiger better than anybody did, and just judging by his body language, I knew he was on some bullshit. He was in the hole, lost all of his profitable Spots, lost all of his respect in the hood, and had two brothers that had recently been murdered in the same month. He had nothing to lose, and turning down a million-dollar deal for Lil' Ole me would have been to good to be true.

(COUPLE DAYS LATER)

I told Madison that I wanted her to join me for a surprise birthday party that was being thrown for Killa Kam, and she agreed to join me. We were on our way to the Banquet Hall where the party was being held when I felt Madison staring at me from the passenger seat. I asked her what she was looking at, "Just you... You know I love you, right?" She asked me. I answered, "Yes, and I love you too, Whasup?". "I been having weird dreams lately... It's been dreams with only you and Ebony in them. Like yall were fighting over me in these dreams. Both of yall were tugging and pulling me toward yall, and I could hear Ebony telling me to come with her because you weren't good for me. I had that dream for two days straight and been trying to figure it out for the court longest and trying to figure out what it means." Madison said. Hearing the details to her dreams were a bit weird, "I don't know what that means, but I wouldn't worry myself about it if I were you. I want you to start relaxing a bit more and eating better than you have been. In only a couple of months, I'm gonna' want to see you walking down the aisle in that all white and telling the 'pastor I do, so you have to be ready. Yah know? I told her with a grin on my face looking at her while I was driving.

Looking confused as if she may have heard wrong, "I do? down the aisle? Are you saying?: Madison asked, turning and staring me in the face. I lifted my shirt where I was hiding the small jewelry box with a smile on my face before pulling over."Madison, I've been in love with you since I first met you. Right then, I told myself that you would be the mother of my child, and now I'm asking you to be my significant other, my wife. I told her with her face in a total shock, eyes filling with tears and gasping for air: "Yes! Yes, I would be your wife". She answered without hesitation. We both dove in each as others arms hugging and kissing in excitement. I then put the four karat diamond ring on her finger, and the look on her face was amazement. Her tears were flowing down her face, and she couldn't stop telling me how much she loved me. It was official. Madison and I were getting married.

"SURPRISE!!" everyone inside the hotel's banquet hall yelled when we entered. The place was decorated in all pink, and what she thought was Killa Kam's surprise

Birthday party actually turned out to be her baby shower. All of her friends, sorority sisters, and family were all in attendance bearing gifts and happy to celebrate the upcoming birth of Our Daughter. Madison looked at me, and her tears began flowing once again, with everything that was going on, she just couldn't help but be overwhelmed. She pulled herself together, and I could see in her face that she couldn't wait to share the good news. "Oh my God, you guys, is this all for me?" She asked, raising her hand, and that had the ring on it up to her face making sure that it was seen. Her friends and family all went crazy and surrounded her to admire the big diamond ring that I had put on her finger.

Killa Kam walked up to Madison, giving her a big hug and kiss on the cheek. He congratulated her on the baby and the wedding and handed her an envelope, He then walked up to me with a smile on his face to give me a play and a hug, "My nigga getting married huh?! Damn, that's crazy."he said in an excited tone. I nodded my head proudly, "Yea, Man, Yo mans growing up your next, watch!" I told him, making even myself laugh. He burst out laughing, "Nawl, not me my dog. Mob wit me real quick so we could celebrate. You gotta have a drink wit' me today, shid you getting married and got a lil one on the way. These are the real reasons they sell drinks by the bottles. To celebrate Killa Kam said we made our way to a table in the back of the Hall. He pulled out and a big bottle of Remy 1738 and poured both of us a glass. He was right; I had every reason to celebrate, and being that all of my ties with Tiger had come to an end, I was really happy. Tiger had called me yesterday, telling me that he no longer needed my services since he was no longer robbing Killa Kam's Uncles. He also told me that I didn't have to worry about our secrets being exposed and told me that he hoped the best for me and my family's future. My connection with Tiger had finally been disconnected, and now I could finally start living how I wanted to. I normally didn't drink, but today I had a reason.

"Killa Kam! Hey Killa Kam," Madison yelled from across the room, getting both of our attention. She held up what looked like a band of money, "Really? Twenty thousand dollars for an unborn child? What am I suppose to do with this? I can't take this.. Madison was saying. He looked at me then back at her, "Shid, that's my Goddaughter in there cooking, and yall is my family. I'm sure you would find something to do with it. Yall ain't seen nothing yet, I'm already looking at cars for her."

Killa Kam replied making the both of us laugh and shake our heads knowing how spoiled our little girl would be. All of Madison's sorrority sisters began smiling and grinning and asking Madison who was Killa Kam. She told them that we were close as brothers. After sitting there drinking for close to an hour and watching Madison open up baby gifts, I was feeling faded. So whasup wit' Uncle Ace and Uncle Body, what them niggas say when Tiger called the deal off that they were suppose to be doing?" I asked Killa Kam. Killa Kam took another big gulp from his glass, "Mmm, all they did was reschedule it." He answered. Thinking I heard him wrong, I asked him to repeat hisself, "They were suppose to meet up yesterday's but Tiger called and rescheduled the meet-up for today instead." He answered. I put the glass of liquor down and tried my best to straighten myself up "Rescheduled it to today? He told me that he cancelled it all together. What time are they pose' to be meeting each other?" I asked.

"Shid, they meeting up today around 5:00-5:30pm. "Whasup?" Killa Kam asked seeing how concerned I was looking. I looked at the time and it was 5:13pm, I panicked knowing that Tiger was on straight bullshit and betraying me once again. He was still planning on robbing Uncle Ace and Uncle Body.

Madison walked up to us telling us that we needed to start loading the truck up with all of the gifts, "What's wrong bro?" Killa Kam asked after seeing the look on my face and the sweat beads rolling down my forehead. "Ummm Baby look, I need you to take the truck, get to your father's house and stay there til' I get there, You hear me?! Killa Kam, c'mon and let's go!" I told the both of them. I stood up stumbling from the liquor we had already consumed. Killa Kam and I ran out of the hotel's doors while Madison yelled my name wondering what was going on.

Killa Kam and I were both faded but it was time for us to pull it together because shit was about to get real in a matter of minutes. I told Killa Kam to call his Uncles to warn them that Tiger was planning on robbing them but after calling them and not getting an answer we assumed that the deal was going down at that moment. I pulled out my phone and made a call myself,

"Hey Hector?"

"Yea, whasup Big Dog?"

" Ummm, not to good but I got some good news for you doe."

"Yo' write down this address, 17383 Hart Street in West Bloomfield." "Yes, that's Tiger's house. I need you right now! I need you to go to that address and lay on him for me and when you get him I need you to hold him. "

"Aight Bro, in a minute." I said before hanging up the phone. Killa Kam told me that his uncle's phones were going straight to the voicemail. I told Killa Kam to takeme to where the deal was being held at and he told me that it was at the old house where I use to live.

I asked Killa Kam if he had this gun on him and he not only had his but had an extra one for me. I was pissed at myself for believing that Tiger wouldn't go through with robbing Killa Kam's uncles for that million dollars.

I told him that they were my people's, and he still didn't give a fuck, he was thinking only about himself and that would make him a dead man soon. I was going to kill Tiger for his betrayal and disloyalty. This would be a body that I would personally enjoy putting six feet underneath the ground.

Gone Bad

We flew through the city to get to my old house and both Killa Kam and myself hoped that his uncles were still alive. I briefed Killa Kam on how and why Tiger was going to rob his uncles and he got as pissed as I was. When we finally pulled up on the block, we seen Tiger's car and Killa's Uncles rental car parked out front of the house. We both jumped out of the car and rushed the front door. I kicked it open and automatically caught a bullet to the shoulder. Looking inside of the house I seen that Tiger had already had Killa's uncles tied up on the floor and shot up holding on to their lives. Tiger seen that it was me and was just about to talk some shit but not before Killa Kam's pistol ripped its bullets through his leg causing him to fall to the floor hiding behind the couch.

"Ya'll not pose to be here Lil' Mello but since yall are I guess yall could join the party!" Tiger yelled. I was ducked off by the kitchen with the kitchen table flipped over in a attempt for it to be some type of shield. Killa Kam was in the living room ducked behind one of the other couches across from where Tiger was. Killa Kam checked to make sure that his Uncles were still alive but no telling for how long. Even though I been shot in the shoulder I was still ready for a gun war.

I peeked out to the living room and seen that Tiger

already had the big bags of a million dollars sitting beside him, "All I know is I can't let you outta here with that money Tiger! As a matter of fact, I can't let you outta! here alive! You gotta' answer for all of the bullshit that you've done before." I told him. Tiger laughed, "All the bullshit that I've done?! Are you fuckin'serious?! What about all the bullshit you done?! You got's to be a Mutha'fuckin' fool if you think I ain't getting out of here with this bag, I'm telling you that right now!!" Tiger yelled back firing shots at the table Iwas ducked behind. "If only you knew all of the shit I done you would've been tried to kill me. Like when I set your brothers up to be killed, they were some fuckin' dummies too. It was so easy! Yall thought I was a fuckin joke so I had to show yall exactly what yall created in me!" I yelled back followed with a couple of shots to where he was hiding. "Well that just breaks my heart to hear Lil' Mello, it really do but I guess we even. I'm the one who sold your O.G that bold dope that caused her to overdose and die. It was so sad watching you go around the neighborhood looking for your mother that was already dead. Don't forget, I'm the one who created you Lil'Mello! I made you nigga!" Tiger yelled before firing more shots at me.

"You didn't create nigga! You didn't make me either! I am my father's son! I was your muscle and if it wasn't for me you wouldn't have been running shit like you have! I yelled back firing more shots at him. Well I guess we both had alot to do with the other but I tell you this, I wont rest until your dead now for getting my brothers killed" Tiger yelled before he stood up and sending at least seven shots at me then another three at Killa Kam before he ran out of the back door. Just when I was about to chase after him I heard Killa Kam's loud moan. I turned around and rushed over to him noticing that he been shot in the arm. I kneeled down asking him if he was alright."I'm good, I'm good.Go get Tiger and that money!" Killa Kam told me.

I told him that I would call for him and his uncles an ambulance then I ran back out the door and Tiger was not in sight.

I then heard a car ramming against another that was coming from the front of the house, I ran up to the front of the house where I seen Tiger ramming his car against Killa Kam's so he could get out of the driveway. Killa Kam's car was blocking Tiger in and at that moment was the best time to attack him. I rushed the car that Tiger was trying to break free but it was to late. He had already made a get away but that didn't stop me from chasing down the car on foot and sending shots through his back window as he drove away.

I stood in the middle of the street tired and pissed that Tiger had gotten away when my phone rang from my pockets. I made my way back to Killa Kam and his uncles when I seen that the person calling my phone was Tiger, "Yo, Lil' Mello, I'm really disappointed in you. I should have let Madison's brothers kill you after you killed Lil' Nate! "

Yes well. I was just calling you to tell on you Imma be outta' town for a while until things die down but you shouldn't worry about me cuz' your gonna' be to busy to worry bout me. I sent your girl Madison a package that's going to blow her mind. In fact, It will blow everybody's minds that's around her. So fuck you I win! As usual!" Tiger said before he hung up. I ran in the house when Killa Kam tossed me the keys to his car telling me that they would be alright because the paramedics were on the way. I told him that I would call and that I had to go and make sure Madison and her family were okay.

In Killa Kam's busted-up car I sped to Madison's father house terrified that my new families life was in danger. I automatically assumed Tiger meant that he sent a bomb to her father's house so I called Madison to warn her but she didn't answer. I hated how she never kept her phone close by her and now that I needed her to answer, I was really worried. I then remembered the tracking program that Tiger had turned me on to when I had to find Madison's friend. I forwarded the program to Hector's phone to assist him on finding Tiger and he texted me that he was on it. I needed Tiger found ASAP and I knew no one wanted him more than Hector did. Hector was for sure to get it done.

Too Late

I turned onto Madison's block, and up ahead, I seen the UPS Truck already pulling away, which meant a package had already been dropped off. I stomped on the gas and parked in front of the house, blocking the street off. When I ran up on the porch, the door was locked, and as I called Madison's name, no one was in a rush to let me in. They all were tuned in to whatever it was that they were watching on the television. Madison's father then answered the door, never taking his eyes off the television. Madison's father, two brothers, and Madison stood in front of the television, looking like zombies, which made me curious to know what it was that they were watching. When I heard my own voice on the television now, it had caught my attention. I stepped inside the house and stood from the front door listening to where my voice was coming from, and what I heard myself saying was a complete shock.

It was a recording between Tiger and myself, where we were discussing some of the many murders that I executed. The ones that stuck out the most was Madison's brother Nate and her best friend Ebony. I couldn't believe Tiger really recorded conversations we had. At the end of the recording, Tiger said that he sent the bloody clothes that I murdered Madison's brother in to The Detroit Homicide Unit, and if her family didn't kill me, then I would for sure do prison time. Madison and the rest of her family turned around to face me, and the pain in her face was a clear expression of the hurt that she was feeling. The tears began rolling down her

face, "Is it true? Romello, tell me that this is some type
of sick prank that Tiger is playing on us? You didn't kill
my brother, did you? Nawl you couldn't have, you didn't
kill Ebony either, did you?"Madison asked, with her
voice cracking from the upcoming tears. I exhaled tired
of all of the secrets that I kept boxed in. I was ashamed
and been ashamed for all the things that I done for a
long time; when I didn't answer and could barely look
her in the face, it made my answer obvious. The look on
all of their faces was filled with anger. They all began to
get antsy moving around in their seats.

Man-Man got so mad and tried stepping closer to me,
but I quickly pulled the pistol from my waist and aiming
at him, telling all of them to stay back. Both brothers
and her father all stepped back, "How could you
Romello?! My brother? My Blood? And my Bestfriend?!
Wow! I been in love with a hitman this whole time."
Madison rhetorically asked while crying at the same
time. The Police sirens began echoing throughout the
neighborhood, which was a clear indication that it was
time for me to leave. "I'm sorry Maddy...I'm sorry for
everything."

I told her as I walked backward out of the house with
my pistol still aimed at her brothers.

The Police sirens sounded like they were getting closer,
Madison and her family stepped out on the porch while I
helped myself in the car. Before pulling off, Madison's
brother Man-Man raised his hand toward me like he
had a pistol in his hand and shooting it at me; I'll catch
you, nigga, you can't run forever!" He threatened. I took

one last look at Madison, who was carrying my baby. "I love you," I said before pulling away from her family's house.

As I drove down the block, there were police cars marked and unmarked coming from both ways, and all stopped at Madison's house. I was sure that they were for me. When I made it away safely from the old neighborhood, the tears again began rolling down my face. I was now a fugitive on the run for multiple murders, and now I was forced to leave my family because some of the poor decisions that I made. I sat at a red light with tears flowing like a baby and me slapping my steering wheel in anger. The car next to me started blowing it's horn to get my attention. I looked over, and it was an old lady waving for me to roll down my window. I then rolled it down to see what it was that she wanted, "Hey Baby, It's gon' be alright you hear me? Whatever you going through it too shall pass, just keep believing in God, and it's going to be alright. Okay Sugar?" She told me with a smile on her face.

She reminded me of the sweet grandmothers from the television that everybody had accent me, " I hear you ma'am thank you." I replied back. She smiled, "Yes, yes. You pull yourself together and keep it pushing, okay? You have yourself a blessed day."She told me before pulling off. I told her to have a good day as well, and I dried the tears from my face pulling off as well.

My phone then rang, and it was Hector telling me some great news, He had Tiger, and they were headed back to Southwest Detroit. I told him that I was on my way.

Before I could head that way, I needed to go and clear my stash out so I could be ready to hit the Highway afterwards. I started laughing because of all the bullshit that been going on in my life; killing Tiger was one of the main things that would make me feel better. I was becoming super light-headed while I was driving, I reached down to my arm when I remembered that I had to been shot. I had lost a lot of blood, and there was blood all over the front seat of the car. My main focus was to just get to my safe then to Southwest, where Tiger was. Hopefully I could make it..

All Get Back In

(11:45pm)

I pulled up in Southwest at Hector's garage, sweating profusely and feeling like shit. The garage was surrounded by Hector's Mexican killers, and I was sure they were already expecting me. When I pulled inside of the huge factory sized garage, I seen Tiger being chained up to the ceiling bloody and beaten badly. I got out and gave Hector a play; he shook his head, taking a look at me, "Whasup brother, good to see you made it. I was worried you wouldn't. You weren't followed, were you?" Hector asked me. "Of course I made it, why wouldn't I ? And Nawl I wasn't followed, why you ask?" I returned the question being a bit confused by his comments. Hector looked back at his crew and then back to me. "You must've haven't seen the television or heard the radio, huh?" He asked to me. I shrugged my shoulders and answered no. "Aww Vato, you're all on the news channel wanted for over twenty murders.

Your not just Detroit's most wanted but Michigan's most wanted. Their calling you the biggest hitman to ever come out of Detroit since your father. I been incarcerated with your father too and didn't even know it till today. He's a cool brother and really respected inside the walls." Hector said sticking his hand out for a handshake. This wasn't just a handshake; it was more like a big sign of respect.

I walked over to Tiger's hanging bloody body when I asked Hector's crew to let him down. They dropped him on the floor when I kneeled down to him. He began to laugh as if he had a reason to, what's so funny nigga?! That you are bout' to die?" I asked him. He laughed harder, "Well, yea, I'll be dead, but your life would be fucked! Your freedom is fucked, I'm sho yo girl, and the same niggas that you were giving plays to in the Club all want you dead! All I wanna' know is, was it worth it?" Tiger asked. I booted Tiger straight to the face ignoring the question that he just asked me. He began laughing again, "I don't care what you do to me or what you say after I'm dead and gone. I still have something to be proud of, and that is that I made you a straight killer like your father!" Tiger said spitting blood from his mouth; Tiger was absolutely right, I had become the killer that I tried my best not to become and because he wanted me to, I did it. What made you go against the street Law you steady embedded into my head about staying loyal and to never ratting out anybody? You not only ratted me out to my girl, but you ratted me out to the police!" I asked

"C'Mon Lil' Mello, I taught you not to rat and to be loyal, but you broke the rules first! You think I didn't know that you were with Shark the night before he came up missing? He told me that if anything happened to him that he was with you last. He sent that to me in a text message. Oh, and you think that I didn't know you had something to do with Pit? I called Madison's father's house because I knew that he knew where you were, and he told me that he just seen you go into Manny's

Club and that you parked behind Pit's car. I'm a lot smarter than you think I am. I must admit, though, your smarter than I expected you to be; I just was smarter, that's all". Tiger told me.

I was surprised to know that he knew as much as he did; I began pacing back and forth, listening to why he betrayed me. But you know what doa? I guess they had it coming. The way how they Gang-Banged your crackhead ass mama before I served her them bold drugs, I guess Karma had to pay them a visit."He said, snatching all of my attention. I stopped pacing back and forth and dove on top of Tiger beating him until I was tired. "Where is she?! Where is

my mother?! Imma' fuckin' kill you!" I yelled, holding him up by his collar. He started laughing, "You could forget about her lil bro, you could never find her burned up body anywhere." He answered.

My eyes watered instantly, thinking of the torture my mother could have suffered. Hector walked over to me, putting his hand on my shoulder and handing a big crowbar, "Beat him to death. It'll make you feel better." He told me. I took the crowbar and repeatedly bashed his face in until he was no longer recognizable, and Hector called my name, telling me to stop. He checked Tiger's pulse, and there wasn't one. After killing Tiger, I flopped in a chair, gasping for my breath. Hector then walked over to me, handing me a big duffle that held the million dollars that Tiger had taken from Killa Kam's Uncles. He told me that Tiger had it in his car when they picked him up.

I reached in my pocket for my phone and called Killa Kam, who was just being released from the hospital from being shot. I started nodding off from feeling light-headed again, but only this time, it was worse from before. I was in pain from my gunshot wound. Hector seen that I wasn't right, and when he approached me, he seen the gunshot wound that I had and asked how long ago did it happen.

I told him hours ago. Hector called one of his uncles over to us; they helped me to a bed that was in the back where I could be helped. Hector said that he would talk to Killa Kam for me and give him directions to where he went. Hector told me that I should relax and get some rest. He assured me that I would be safe as long as I was in his presence.

On The Run

(4 AM)

I woke up with a patched-up arm, and standing over me was Hector, his Uncles, Killa Kam, Uncle Ace, and all of the rest of the Mexican crew were standing from afar. I was hooked up to I.V's like I was in a hospital and felt a bit better than I did before. Hector told me that I had lost a lot of blood, but now I was better since I had some treatment. "Whasup Man, you in some deep shit now, huh bro?" Killa Kam said to me with a grin on his face. I just shook my head, "Yea, Madison will never talk to me again. Yo Ace, I got yall money back. My mans Hector here went and picked Tiger up for me. I told him. Uncle Ace told me that he had already heard and just insisted that I got more rest.

"I wanna' thank you for coming to try and stop the deal from happening. It's unfortunate we lost my Brother Body, but this is the life that we chose. We all gon' be alright after this shit." Uncle Ace told me. "Look, look on the sun look... Again Papi! One of the Little Mexicans sitting in front of the T.V yelled for our attention. My face was on the television with a big wanted signal above my head and under my picture It was titled, "DETROIT'S TOP PAID HITMAN and that I was wanted for a twenty thousand dollar reward. The Media was telling everything about me from my incarcerated father down to me being a student at Michigan State University. They were even interviewing people that were in my classes trying to get them to describe the type of person that I was. I sat up and started unhooking all that was connected to me, "Well, Boys, I think it's time I got up outta here being that I'm wanted all over the place. It was an honor dealing with all of you ." I told them as I began putting my clothes back on. "Where you going, Bro?" Killa Kam asked. I shrugged my shoulders, answering that I didn't know where I was going. "I could hide you good out in Cali, I could get you a new identity and all, even new fingerprints but you would have to get out there on your own. That's the least that I could do for you. I may even have a few jobs for you out there." Uncle Ace told me. When he told me he had jobs, I was sure that he was talking about, he had some people that needed to be killed. "Hmmm, I'll most definitely call. I replied back when I get out there. That don't sound like a bad idea.

I stood up when Killa Kam gave me a Play and a Man-hug, "Be smooth, my dog makes sure that you stay under the radar. Madison and your daughter will be just fine, so don't worry about them. As long as I'm straight then they would be good forever. Imma' take care of them like family." He promised me. He then handed me the keys to the Commander truck telling me that it was his low-key ride, and it had a hemi just in case I needed to make a quick getaway from something. Uncle Ace gave me a play and a Man-hug telling me to call him soon as I got to California. I then turned to Hector, and he gave me a Play and a Man-hug as well and telling me to call him when or if I ever needed him. I told him that I would and thanked him for everything that he has done for me.

I hopped in the Commander where all of my belongings that I had packed up from my Safehouse were sitting in the back seat. I looked at all of them while the garage door was opening, and I saluted them before pulling away.I never thought that I would ever be saying good-bye to people under these circumstances, but if I didn't want to go to prison, then this was the only way to stay free. I never thought I would be forced to leave Detroit but like how Uncle Ace said, "THIS IS THE LIFE THAT WE CHOSE.," and I had to live with all of the decisions that I ever made. I drove down the street, leaving all of my bad decisions and regrets in the rear-view and was headed toward a new beginning.

Finale

ONE YEAR LATER,

MCKENZIE'S FIRST BIRTHDAY

Sitting in an SS Trailblazer truck a half block away from Madison's house, I used my binoculars to watch my daughter celebrate her first birthday party spot that was outside in the backyard. She was the prettiest little girl that I ever saw and her mother Madison was still as beautiful as ever. Being that I was on the run for the past year, I was unable to visit my daughter, so she hadno clue who I was, but what Killa Kam would try and teach her. I tried calling Madison many times, but she would always ignore my calls then go and change her number. With all of the new technology that I was in possession of, there was no way that she could hide from me. Even with all of the pain that I caused Madison, I still had a feeling that deep down in her heart, she still loved me like I loved her. It was clear that she wasn't forgiving me for all of the murders I committed, nor was she trying to hear anything that I had to say but trip every blue moon when I would call, sometimes she would just hold the phone. I think she was doing it so I could hear our daughter play in the background.

xxx

Two houses down from Madison were an FBI unmarked car parked surveilling the house just in case I ever got stupid and wanted to visit.

Madison hated how they stay watching over her and often tried to get them to leave, but they told her as long as I was on the run that they would always be watching. One thing that was surprising about Madison was that she never testified on me or wrote a statement on anything that she knew that I was involved in, which showed her loyalty toward me was real. I saw Killa Kam coming from inside the house with a big birthday cake and placing it on the Sun table. He had been the best Godfather possible to have and kept his word by making sure that he treated both Madison and Mekanzle like they were his family. Killa Kam and I talked often, but we had to be very careful how often we did talk to avoid the calls being tracked and tapped.

Killa Kam was indeed a true friend because just being involved with me slowed his money up because now they were watching him. He didn't mind, though because he was already rich anyway. He would buy at least three different phones every month just so we could talk, and he could tell me about my daughter. He uses to record McKenzie playing and would send the video footage to me so I could see how much she was growing.

After Mckenzie blew out her one candle and put her hands in the cake, her mother began opening up her gifts. Killa Kam insisted that she opened up the two gifts that he just handed her first. Inside one of the boxes was a phone and a card that read "FROM DADDY," Madison seen the phone inside of the box, and through my binoculars, I could see Killa Kam telling her to turn it on.

?

Right at that moment I called the phone and Madison answered. I just stared at her and didn't say anything. Madison stood up and began looking all around the neighborhood as if she was looking for me. When I looked at the FBI Agents, I could l that they were wondering who it was that she was looking for they grabbed their binoculars too and began looking around hoping to find me out, "McKenzie, come here, baby. Say hi to Da-Da." Madison told our daughter. My mouth dropped, hearing her tell our little girl that. I then saw Stone and Man-Man's attention captured when they heard what their sister just told their neice. They both stood up and stepped outside the backyards gate walking separate directions to look for me. I reached on the side of my seat for my Desert Eagle. Even though I was far enough away, I still had to been prepared or anything. I then heard my daughter's little voice through the phone, "Hi." she said. My heart damn near melted when I heard her speak. "Hi, Baby, Da-Da loves you," I told her with the binoculars still on her. A big smile had spread across her little face before she ran away, and I couldn't believe it. Madison put the phone back up to her ear, remaining silent, "I'm sorry....I still love you." I whispered to her before hanging up.

The FBI Agents were going crazy, and I could tell that they knew it was me on the other end of the phone. Stone ran up behind his sister, snatching the phone from her, but he was already too late. I saw Killa Kam walk over to the FBI Agents and began talking to them. I then started my truck and slowly cruised up the block with my tinted windows rolled all the way up.

I bent the corner passing the FBI Agents, Man-Man, who was walking up the block looking for me, I was slowly passing the corner house where Madison lived. She stared at the dark-tinted truck that I was in and smiled as if she knew it was me, "We love you too." She mouthed to me as I kept riding past.

I smiled and quickly typed a message in the text message part of the burnout phone that I had and tossed it out of the window. When I got halfway down the block, I saw the FBI Agent through my rear-view mirror step in the middle of the street picking the phone up. The message I put in the phone said, "YOU JUST MISSED ME!LOL". I turned another corner, only imagining how mad they all were that I was just up under their noses, and they couldn't catch me.

As I hopped back on the Highway, I looked in my rear-view and seen that I still had a smile on my face after hearing my daughter speak to me. I lost my family, college, career plans, and freedom. I felt like a Slave that was on the run, and all I could do was ask myself was, "Was all the money and acceptance from others really worth it?". The answer was no; it wasn't worth it because now all I had was money, and there was no telling how long I would have it before getting caught.

My phone rang, and it was Uncle Ace that was out in California telling me that he had another job for me. "Aight fasho', I'll be back in town in a couple of days. How much we talking bout'?" I asked. Uncle Ace told me that this particular body would get me fifty thousand dollars, "Yea I'm sure I could squeeze that one into my

⍰

schedule." I told him. I reached in my middle console for my big boy Cartier Glasses and threw them on my face, I'm still about that Money doe no matter what!" I said to myself after hanging up the phone and flying down the highway......

To Be Continued...

Made in the USA
Middletown, DE
05 June 2022

66550934R00142